RANSOM CREEK REMAINS

ADAM SADLER
BRADY J. SADLER

For Field Training Officer Nate Rock.

You were the only ballplayer I ever wanted to share catcher duties with.

Thank you for serving and protecting, buddy.

Your friend always,

Brady

For Amelia.

You're my favorite person in the world.

Ever since you were born, you've inspired everything I do.

Love, your father,

Adam

Also by Brady J. Sadler
www.bradyjsadler.com

The Days of Astasia
Eve of Corruption (2012)

The Malice of Light
The Acrid Sky (2023)
The Withered Roots (2024)
The Smoldering Vein (Forthcoming)

In Short Order (2025)
Emerald Decay (2025)

Relic Meyers
Relic Meyers & The Rhythms of Ruin (2024)
Relic Meyers & The Harmony of Hexes (2025)

Prologue

Madison Avery didn't want to drink what remained in the can, but she tipped it back regardless. While the beer was warm, she welcomed the sting in her throat as it went down—it took her mind off the divorce.

"Whoa, slow down, girl!"

After draining the rest of her third drink, Madison returned her gaze to Cassandra; the girl's green eyes widened in delighted shock. That reaction gave Madison some bizarre sense of accomplishment, as if getting drunk was some special skill.

But if Madison's mother had taught her anything, it was that putting back drinks was one of the few reliable coping mechanisms for living in Ransom Creek.

Madison tossed the empty can over her shoulder, causing a hollow clatter on the patio stones. "You gonna finish yours?"

Cassandra flinched at that, but handed over her nearly untouched beer anyway. When Madison reached for it, she noticed a slight recoil at the last minute. Knowing her friend didn't approve of her getting hammered had a strange effect on Madison, and she threw her head back dramatically again to chug the beer in defiance.

A shout came from the upper deck overlooking the Windsors' backyard: "Avery!"

Madison kept her eyes clenched as several lines of warm, watered-down alcohol trickled down her chin and neck. She heard the footsteps descending the stairs and recognized Cliff Windsor's voice amongst the laughter of his friends. But she just kept drinking, hoping to dull the party and drown out any thoughts of her broken family.

"You better hope your dad doesn't show up," Cliff joked. Despite the nastiness in his voice, Madison was still madly in love with him and wanted to impress him. So she put on a show, twirling drunkenly as she polished off her fourth can of Keystone Light.

"Cassie, how many has she had?" Elijah sounded concerned. "Her dad's a cop, man."

"He's a detective," Jared replied, just before unleashing a belch that unsettled Madison's stomach. "Donnie can't do shit unless she gets caught embezzling money or something"—another powerful burp—"like your mom, Eli."

"She didn't do that," Elijah snapped. "And you know it, Larson!"

Madison's vision was blurry when she finally opened her eyes, tossing the empty can aside. The alcohol was certainly working now, which was a small relief given how much it tasted like piss. She saw Eli, Jared, Cliff, and Valerie circling her and Cassie. Eli was turned toward Jared, Sheriff Larson's all-star quarterback son. The smaller boy was trying to look imposing, but even through her beer goggles Madison could tell he was scared trying to stand up to someone of Jared's social caliber.

"Whatever," Jared said, turning his cold blue eyes back on Madison. "I just mean Don Avery's not going to roll up here and bust up a high school party. He's probably reading cold case files from back when Nixon was in office. Right, Maddie?"

All eyes turned to her, and Madison felt a deep resentment for her father in that moment, as if Donald Avery was responsible for everything that evening: the divorce, her drinking, her mom's drinking, her friends mocking his job—all of it.

"Yeah," Maddie said, her voice sounding muddled and distant against the growing pressure in her ears. "He's probably finally writing that report about Darlene McCoy's garden gnome that kept getting vandalized."

This drew a round of chuckles, easing the tension. But only for a moment.

A wolf howled nearby, jolting the teens.

They all looked toward the hill that sloped away from the Windsors' back lawn toward the dark ravine. Music still rattled the basement windows where about a dozen other teens were smoking pot and making out, but the animal's echoing cry had overpowered it.

"That sounds way too close," Valerie whispered. Despite her own fright, Madison couldn't help but notice her romantic rival clinging to Cliff for protection.

"Sounded like a wolf," Cassie said, hooking her arm through Madison's.

"Can't be," Jared replied. His voice sounded less commanding than usual; not scared, but also not confident. "Not with all these lights and the music. Would never get that close—not a wolf."

The howl came again. Whatever produced it held the bestial sound out longer this time, as if to mock the teens.

"We should get inside," Elijah suggested. "Whatever that is, it's very fucking close."

The tail end of the howl was cut short with a sudden pathetic whimper. The silence that followed created a vacuum between the teens, each of them looking to the other for some sort of explanation.

Before anyone could come up with a reason for the eerie happening, a shadow took shape from the distant trees, drawing a gasp from Cassie.

"Who's that?" Valerie asked, still grabbing onto Cliff as if he were Superman. Madison seethed, despite the terror that gripped her.

The figure emerging from the ravine held each of them enthralled—a ghost returning to a home besieged by the modern world.

"Hey!" Jared broke away from the circle, stalking toward the hill where the stranger was climbing. "This is private property!"

"I thought it was a party."

The voice sounded unnaturally close in relation to the silhouette's distance, which continued its approach, immune to Jared's machismo. Despite the night's warmth, a chill fingered its way down Madison's spine as she watched the newcomer step into the deck floodlight.

"Hey, Rachel," Elijah called out. "I didn't think you'd make it."

Madison clearly heard Valerie hiss at her pot supplier. "You invited a Kraft to the party?"

"The more the merrier," Cliff said loudly and defiantly. "Want a beer, new girl?"

"I'm not that new," Rachel replied. She held her right arm across her stomach, gripping her left elbow guardedly. The expression on her face didn't match her shy posture; she challenged Jared with those cold eyes framed in heavy black eyeliner.

"New enough not to know to stay out of the ravine at night." Jared snorted and spat into the grass. "You hear that wolf out there?"

"I thought it couldn't be a wolf?" Cassie remarked.

Jared ignored her, still stalking toward Rachel. "You know what happens to girls in the ravine, right?"

Those words seemed to deepen the cold that crept into Madison's bones. Something was eerily familiar about this odd turn of events.

"Wasn't there supposed to be a bonfire?" Rachel surveyed the back yard, looking lost.

Jared turned around to look at the others, frowning in confusion. "What are you talking about?"

The howl came again, eliciting a gasp from both Cassie and Valerie. Even as her own heart stuttered in response, Madison noticed Rachel looked unbothered—almost bored.

"We should get inside," Eli said. "Whatever's out there is harshing my buzz."

As they all turned to head back inside, Madison held her gaze on Rachel. Something about the girl's detached nature reminded Madison of what happened earlier that day at school. The feeling of déjà vu she felt earlier now made sense.

"I'm sorry about what happened," Madison said, keeping her voice low so her friends wouldn't hear—they were partially responsible. "At lunch...that—It wasn't cool."

Rachel stared at her without emotion. Those cold dark eyes were like a raven's, calculating someone's imminent demise. And then something happened that nearly made Madison gasp.

She smiled.

Rachel Kraft, the new girl from the only trailer park in Ransom Creek who barely engaged with any other teens, smiled at Madison.

Not knowing how to process that, Madison turned to join her friends, who loudly made their way to the basement doors. The howl that came from the ravine didn't surprise them this time—it certainly didn't surprise Madison, who was still wrestling with the ghost of Rachel Kraft's terrifying smile.

Elijah slid the basement's glass door open for them. "You coming, Rachel?"

The howl ended again with a sudden yelp, followed by a pathetic whimper.

This time they all turned around, but Rachel Kraft was gone.

CHAPTER 1
UNREPORTED

D etective Sergeant Donald Avery used to like Mondays. The start of a week had a distinct lack of chaos, and it provided an ordered person—like himself—a momentary refrain from sifting through three or four days of mental debris.

But the manila envelope that sat in his car's passenger seat contained over thirteen years' worth of debris that Donald had to contend with, and he now no longer liked Mondays.

His normal routine was further disrupted by the mere fact that he was driving himself to the Ransom Creek Police Station. He had grown accustomed to riding shotgun with his partner, Anne Warren, which is what he had done up until last Wednesday. But her sudden retirement added one more wrinkle to Donald's normally ordered schedule.

Regardless, he thumbed the radio dial to turn up the dispatch chatter, hoping work might take his mind off the uneasy start to the week.

Beth Hampton's monotone voice came through: "Unit 214, report of a downed stop sign at the corner of Hawthorne and Mill. Public Works notified, but check for traffic hazard."

An officer whose voice Donald didn't recognize was quick to respond. "Copy. En route."

Another riveting day, Donald thought, lowering the radio volume back down as another patrol dispatch came in. It'd been about a week or two since his department was last dispatched, and it was far from urgent.

However, it had led to his partner's abrupt career change, leaving Donald stuck with some transfer from the city.

Turning down Cambridge Avenue, he glanced over at the passenger seat again. The wretched documents that had been so kindly left on his apartment stoop first thing that morning looked so much like any other report he would turn in to the clerk. Without breaking the seal on the thing, Donald knew exactly what it contained, and he would put off opening it as long as he could.

"Yo!"

Donald slammed on the brakes. Even though he hadn't even been touching the gas, the car still jerked to an abrupt stop. In front of his pristine Ford Crown Victoria was a disheveled manchild in tattered jeans and a green work jacket. He held his arms out in the universal sign of *What the hell?*

Annoyed but ashamed, Donald held up a hand to accept fault—he had been more focused on his failed marriage than the road. But the mustached man just jammed his middle finger in response and finished crossing the street while drinking his coffee.

"Seems about right," Donald said with a sigh and a grim shake of his head. The car behind him barked its horn and Donald took his foot off the brake, finishing his turn toward his regular coffee stop on the corner of Cambridge and Parkview.

Checking the time, he was relieved to see he had about twenty minutes before he had to be at the station. Even though his daughter rarely wanted to spend more than ten minutes alone with him, Donald would take whatever he could get, especially since the separation.

Madison sat alone in Creekside Coffee, vacantly staring at her untouched croissant. She didn't look up, but Donald was sure she noticed his arrival. At seventeen, Maddie was much the same as she was at thirteen: determined to never appear eager to see her father.

"Morning, Detective. The usual?"

Donald nodded to Hank behind the counter. "I'll take a plain bagel too. Toasted, no cream cheese."

"You got it," Hank replied.

Donald pulled out the chair across from his daughter. "You're early today." As he heard the words come out of his mouth, an unsettling thought occurred to him. Did Laura have their daughter drop off the divorce papers? Was that why it looked like she had been here for a while, waiting for him? Donald clenched his teeth as he sat down; he didn't want to take any frustrations out on Madison.

She picked at her croissant, still not meeting his gaze. "I had to do some stuff before school."

Like acting as your mom's courier, he thought, but just smiled and tapped the table between them. "Senior year... Can you believe it? This time next year you'll be starting college."

Madison shrugged, finally glancing up at her dad. "It's just Branson—it's not like I'm going far."

Hank dropped off Donald's breakfast and then slipped away without saying a thing. "Well," Donald replied, "that's not what I meant. It's just—I'm glad you'll still be nearby, but it's still a big change."

A cold silence fell between them in which Donald noticed his daughter's gaze drifting out the huge window overlooking Parkview Avenue. Given his job, he knew how to read people, and something was certainly occupying Madison's thoughts.

"So," he said, blowing on his coffee. "Have you given much more thought about what you want to major in?"

Her eyes fell on him. "Dad, do you know much about the Krafts?"

The question sent a chill through Donald, despite the warm beverage he held with both hands. "You talking about the new girl at your school? Rebecca?"

"Rachel," Madison corrected.

Donald glanced over his shoulder. The coffee shop was bustling near the counter, with many of the familiar faces lined up for their morning caffeine fix. But none of those customers paid the Averys any attention—if any of them did, they likely wouldn't hear a conversation over the din near the register.

"You probably know more about her than I do," Donald offered, taking a sip of coffee. "I know her mom has a couple DUIs and I think she might have spent a couple nights sleeping it off in the sheriff's station since they moved back. Other than that, what's there to know?"

He hoped by keeping the discussion current he could avoid any more difficult discussions about Caroline Kraft's mysterious death in 1974, but he would be quite shocked if Madison knew anything about a cold case from twenty years ago.

No one in town talked about Caroline Kraft anymore, Donald Avery included.

Madison tore off a piece of croissant but didn't eat it. "Everyone seems to act like they know something terrible about the Kraft family, but whenever I ask..." She finally put the piece of pastry in her mouth and stared at her father as she chewed.

Donald took another sip of coffee. Another silence fell between them.

"Did you come by my apartment this morning?"

The last twenty years of watching guilty people hide things from him told Donald everything he needed to know about Madison's reaction. He was certain she had dropped off the divorce papers, which meant she knew.

"Mom said it'd be easier for all of us." She averted her eyes again, poking her flaking breakfast. "Said she couldn't do it herself, and didn't want to have some court official bringing it by like in the movies."

"You couldn't have just given it to me?" Donald's calm facade almost fell away when she looked up at him again, her dark eyes glistening with barely restrained tears. He felt oddly guilty, like he was grilling her, but really, he just wanted to make sure she was okay with all of this. He wanted to be there for her.

The phone rang, drawing Madison's attention as if it were an alarm.

"I need to get to school, Dad." She reached to get her bag and pushed the small plate of uneaten food toward him.

Donald pushed back the chair to get up. "Let me drive you, hon. We can talk about this."

"Hey, Detective," Hank called from across the counter. "Bethany's on the line. Says to turn your radio on. Sounds like she's got a live one."

"See ya, Dad."

Madison slipped past Donald as he took a quick bite of his dry bagel. He tossed the rest in the trash as he followed her out the door, trying not to spill his coffee in his haste.

"We should talk, Maddie. I know this isn't—"

"I don't want to talk," Madison snapped, glaring at him over her shoulder. "I had to talk to Mom all weekend about this and I'm sick of hearing about it! Alright?"

Donald felt the eyes of familiar strangers on him as they passed in and out of Creekside Coffee. He stared dumbly at his daughter's back as she swiftly crossed the street on her way to school. Donald watched until she disappeared around the corner.

When he finally got in his car and turned the engine on, Beth was on the radio asking for him.

"Your new partner's here looking for you, Don. City boy. Says he wants to start the case without you."

Donald grabbed the radio mic. "Partner?" He hadn't been informed of a new partner starting today—there's no way the transfer would have come through already. "What case?"

"We got a missing person routed from the sheriff's office," Beth explained. "Apparently it went unreported over the weekend. Subject's mother is specifically requesting a detective."

He pressed the mic, began to ask who it was, then hesitated and let go. The same chill he felt from Madison's question went through him.

"It's Tori Kraft."

CHAPTER 2
THE WRONG FOOT

Detective Edward "Eddie" Rane couldn't help but smile as the sheriff led him to an empty interrogation room. Aside from almost getting run over by some banker, his morning had been off to a pretty decent start. Then, not five minutes after getting to the office and finding his desk, he already felt like he had stepped in the proverbial shit when the sheriff asked him to talk privately for a minute.

But he didn't let this unexpected plot twist get him down. Ever since Little League, he loved getting thrown a curveball—they made the hits feel all the sweeter.

Ransom Creek wasn't exactly what Eddie had expected when the transfer came in. After everything that happened in Charlotte, he figured the brass would try to stick him in a retirement community down in Florida. But walking the two miles from his tiny Parkview apartment to the station gave Eddie something he couldn't remember having since he was a teenager.

A sense of calm.

Patrick Larson, however, *was* exactly what Eddie had expected: a small-town high school golden boy who had probably inherited the position of Ransom Creek sheriff from his old man. He was a solidly built dude without a patch of hair on his face, and he smelled like a clothing catalog might convince you a lumberjack smells like.

Eddie followed him into the small room and took a seat.

"You sure I can't get you some coffee?" Sheriff Larson asked, without the slightest hint of generosity in his gravelly voice. He took a sip of his own from the plain white mug as he took a seat across from Eddie.

Eddie just grinned for another long beat, meeting the man's icy glare with the same detached attention he might have given a yellow traffic light. "I'm good—stopped at Hank's place on Parkview. Much better drip than I'm used to in the city." Leaning over the table that separated them, he added, "What I really want—and no offense, obviously—is to get this over with."

Larson's left eye twitched. "Pardon?"

"Come on." Eddie leaned back, crossing his arms. "We both know what this is: my transfer blindsided you, and here you are on my first day, ready to swing your dick in my face so I know whose jurisdiction this is—let's just cut the foreplay."

Patrick's eyes narrowed, but only slightly. "You don't strike me as the type of guy that would take the hint, regardless of what I swing in front of your face."

Eddie snorted a laugh. "My reputation precedes me. Look, I think we're both pretty sour about my being here, but for the sake of both our hairlines, how about we just stay out of each other's way?" He began to get up.

"Do you think I don't know, Detective?"

Eddie froze. The sheriff's voice had an edge to it that felt like a knife to his throat. *How could he know?* Eddie couldn't help but glance at the small window set in the door. *No wonder he brought me in here,* he thought, easing himself back into his chair as he settled his eyes back on Larson. "They told me it wouldn't be on my record."

"It's not." Larson smiled before taking another sip. He let Eddie sweat before adding, "Nothing comes into my town without me knowing.

This isn't Charlotte, son, and I'm not a senator giving you a slap on the wrist for snooping on his boy. No one in Ransom Creek wants your kind here, so let me tell you how things are going to work."

Even though he had to bite his lower lip, Eddie kept silent. It wouldn't do any good to push the town's top cop any further on his first day.

"You stick to the job," Larson continued. "Petty theft and vandalism are going to be your bread and butter here in Ransom Creek, we'll handle the rest. This place will treat you as well as you treat it. So ditch those rags you're wearing and get a haircut. Buy a real suit too. Folks 'round here won't respect some dirtbag grunge-head," he motioned to Eddie's green jacket, matching high top sneakers, and jeans, "or whatever you call this get-up."

"You got it, pops," Eddie said flatly, ready for the bizarre encounter to be over.

Sheriff Larson left the interrogation room. Eddie spent almost five minutes afterward staring at the man's empty white mug, wondering just how much of the Charlotte situation the Ransom Creek Sheriff's Department knew about.

An hour ago, Eddie thought he had lucked out—not everyone that tangles with a US senator is fortunate enough to get a fresh start. But now he felt like he was in deeper hot water than before, and it was only day one.

A pimple-faced rookie opened the door, recoiling slightly. He clearly expected to find someone with shorter hair, a clean shave, and a pressed suit.

"Hey, uh... Are you Detective Rane?"

Eddie stood up. "See any other grunge-heads in the area?"

"You're Donald Avery's new partner, right? He's usually here by now, but dispatch hasn't been able to reach him. We got a mom up front looking for her daughter."

The kid led Eddie down the short hall of interrogation rooms toward the front lobby where a woman's frantic voice carried over the dispatch chatter.

"—I just saw him leave! Can't you call him back?"

"I'm sorry, Mrs. Kraft," a young woman replied, "the sheriff isn't available this morning, but we'll get our detectives on your case right away."

"You rang," Eddie said, pushing the short partition door aside as he stepped out into the lobby. A young woman in a ratty Kiss shirt turned to face him. Despite the frantic energy she gave off, Eddie was slightly stunned by how pretty she was.

"Excuse me," she said, turning back to the dispatcher whom Eddie had met just fifteen minutes ago. "When can I talk to a detective then?"

"This is Detective Rane," Beth Hampton explained. "Once his partner gets here, they can take your statement." She stood up and looked at Eddie over her computer monitor. "Just spoke with Avery, he'll be here in five."

Even though the rational side of Eddie's mind knew that he should wait for his new partner, the sight of a damsel in distress pulled at the core of why he wanted to get into law enforcement in the first place. His heroic instincts took over.

"Let him know where we are when he gets here. Come on back, Mrs. Kraft," Eddie said, giving Beth a confirming wave while holding the partition open for his first case in Ransom Creek. "Let's grab a quiet room back here and you can fill me in."

"Um, Detective," Beth began, but her attention turned to the ringing phone.

Eddie led Mrs. Kraft back toward one of the station's two interview rooms. He held the door open and motioned for her to have a seat.

"It's Tori," she said.

"Huh?"

She looked at him with troubled yet dazzling eyes. "My name's Tori."

He smiled as he closed the door. "Eddie. Sorry for the hold up, Tori. I understand your daughter's missing?" He pulled the notebook out of his jacket pocket. "She didn't come home last night?"

"She didn't come home Friday night."

Eddie looked up to see Tori's eyes narrow.

"Which is what I told the sheriff's office on Saturday afternoon."

Looking over his shoulder as if Sheriff Larson were peering in through the door's window, Eddie asked, "You already reported her missing and no one's been assigned?"

Tori took a deep, ragged breath. "This isn't the first time Rachel's disappeared. They think I'm overreacting—like I should just wait it out again. But it's their job to at least look, right? Last time I reported her missing she was only gone for a night. Before that, it was just the afternoon she skipped school when we first moved here. But still—they should be looking for her, right?"

We'll handle the rest, Sheriff Larson had said. Eddie clenched his fist, imagining that asshole pushing this woman's report aside if it didn't fall in line with whatever perception he wanted for his community.

The vision Eddie had of Ransom Creek that morning—a peaceful pocket tucked into the Appalachians—was already curdling thanks to the man in charge. But looking into Tori's worried eyes, he tried to provide the calming presence someone in her condition would likely need.

"Let's start from the beginning." He motioned for her to speak. "I'll handle your case personally, but I want a full picture, alright? Now, what's your daughter's full name and age?"

Tori seemed to grow calmer. "Rachel Abigail Kraft. Seventeen."

"And has she ever not come home before?"

After a brief silence, Eddie looked up to see her raising an eyebrow at him. "You haven't been here long, have you?"

Before he could reply, the door swung open and Eddie was greeted by a banker in a striking blue suit. The man looked familiar, but before Eddie could figure out why, the intruder turned from Tori to give Eddie a puzzled look of annoyance.

"I'm sorry... Are you Mr. Kraft?"

Eddie looked at Tori, who seemed as confused as he was. But when he looked back at the man in the blue suit, his hands were on his hips, now revealing the badge on his belt.

Snorting a laugh, Eddie motioned for his new partner to sit in the seat next to him. "My partner here is a bit of a joker, Tori. As I was about to say, this is my first day, but—"

"When was the last time you saw her?" Donald interrupted, moving the chair next to Eddie to the head of the table before sitting down and producing his own, much nicer notebook.

Oh, we know who's in charge now, Eddie thought.

Tori looked down at her jagged fingernails, each adorned with the remnants of dark polish. "Friday morning. I had to work that night, so I just saw her before school."

"Does she have any after-school activities?" Eddie asked, drawing an aggravated glance from the senior detective. *The car!* Eddie remembered.

This dick almost ran me over, and now he's acting like I just kissed his wife because I kicked off a case without him.

Tori looked at Donald as if needing permission to reply. "No. She keeps to herself. We just moved back at the end of last school year, so she doesn't have a lot of friends or anything."

"And you've already taken this up with the sheriff's office," Donald began.

"But we'll take it from here," Eddie offered, flipping his notebook closed. "Let us get a few things together, and we'll be in touch."

"We'll need to take a detailed statement," Donald instructed. "Could you give us a minute? Someone from the desk will get the full report form started with you."

Moving to escort her out to the lobby, Eddie did his best to avoid Donald Avery's gaze, but he felt it regardless.

"I have to work tonight," Tori explained, reaching into her purse and pulling out a scrap of paper and a pen. "I'll be here until around eleven." She jotted down the name and number to what Eddie assumed was a bar. When she handed it to him, she gave him a smile that made Eddie think of all those old detective movies he watched as a kid where the dame charmed the gruff old private eye. "Thank you, Detective Rane."

"Eddie," he said with a smile. "We'll talk soon, Tori. Let us know if Rachel calls or anything."

He watched her disappear around the corner toward the lobby before he turned to face the music.

Donald Avery stood in the doorway, his jaw tight and his blank eyes holding an icy gaze on Eddie.

"I never thought they'd partner me up with such a reckless driver," Eddie said with a smile, extending his hand toward Donald. "Detective Eddie Rane. Looking forward to cracking this case with you."

"I'll be in the chief's office." Donald turned and left Eddie hanging.

With a sardonic smile, Eddie mumbled under his breath, "Really starting off on the right foot here, buddy."

CHAPTER 3
EARLY CHECKOUT

M arcus Vandrel wasn't a man accustomed to waiting. As the wealthiest resident in Ransom Creek, he had Mayor Schaffer on speed dial and had a permanent reserved table at just about every decent restaurant across South Carolina.

However, given the fact that he was actively being blackmailed, Marcus sat with his legs crossed in the uncomfortable chair that seemed to swallow his small frame. He regarded the hotel lobby with a mix of nostalgia and resentment.

The Brookridge Lodge hadn't changed in decades—the same polished cherrywood floors covered disparately in tacky rugs, the same stone hearth crackling year round with a fire that was more for ambience than heat. The same overstuffed leather chairs—like the one currently digesting him—arranged with the sort of calculated disorder that made the place feel homey to tourists but artificial to him.

Even the scent lingered: a blend of pine cleaner and old books, maybe something floral masked beneath. Marcus hated how memory lived in the details, because he didn't want to remember, and the long wait to meet his blackmailer gave him far too much time to consume the minutiae of the place.

Velvet curtains were drawn across the corridors to either side of the lobby. A painting of the ridge line that once hung in Roger Dupree's den now presided over the front desk. The ridiculous stuffed bear still stood sentinel near the desolate entrance.

Marcus hadn't set foot in the Brookridge since 1974, and the place hadn't so much welcomed him back as it had recognized him, beckoning him to reminisce about the bloody affair that was birthed from the Brookridge's basement.

He shivered, shifting in his chair as if a change of perspective would keep those deeper memories at bay.

"Marcus?"

Now he twisted in the opposite direction to see none other than Brookridge's balding owner and operator striding toward him from the low-lit bar. Roger Dupree wore a shocked smile on his face, affixing his hands on his hips like some sort of jovial mother who caught their child doing something equal parts mischievous and adorable.

"Please tell me you're here to finally talk about that investment. I still can't believe you'd fund that trailer park on the outskirts while I'm over here promising triple on the return."

Roger had been relentlessly pestering Marcus to invest in a new hotel on the north side of the creek, yet while it was an excellent business proposal, Marcus had more pressing matters on his mind. However, since Roger clearly didn't know who was staying in his hotel, Marcus used the assumed pretext to his advantage.

"Actually, Roger, I am," Marcus said, slowly pushing himself out of the deepening chair. "I thought it would be prudent to come see your operation if we were to pursue such a venture."

Roger clapped his hands, producing a sharp sound that started the front desk clerk and echoed across the lobby's vaulted ceiling. "Great to hear! It's about time you came to visit—Christ, I don't think I've seen you here since..." The joy melted from Roger's face as his eyes sank to the floor, as if looking into the void of the hotel's lower levels. But he recovered quickly, flashing Marcus an artificial smile. "Should we go to my office and chat?"

Marcus looked up at the lobby's clock. Jonathan was almost an hour late now, and he wondered if the man would even show his traitorous face. The momentary thought crossed Marcus' mind that maybe the man lost the stomach for extortion, but he doubted that was the case.

Jonathan Keene was nothing if not persistent.

"Let me take a look around first," Marcus said, feigning an examination of the place. Even if he got into business with Roger, he wanted no part in the actual operations or design of a new hotel, but this particular charade gave him the perfect excuse to confront his old friend; if he were, in fact, even here.

"Sure thing," Roger said, motioning toward the desk. "Claire will help you out with anything. Just come on back to my office when you're ready to buckle down on this."

Marcus waited until the man was out of sight before approaching the front desk. The woman whose name tag said *Claire* smiled brightly.

"Good morning, how can I help you?"

"I was hoping you might be able to tell me about one of your guests," Marcus began, feeling in his pocket for his money clip. "He was supposed to meet me down here for breakfast this morning and I'm afraid he may have forgotten."

Claire reached for the phone. "I can call his room if you like—"

Marcus held a hand up to stop her. "I was actually hoping you might be able to tell me which room he's in. I'd like to give him a little surprise, that bonehead, for forgetting our appointment. His name is Jonathan Keene."

The woman pushed a shock of blonde hair off her brow as she offered him an apologetic grin. "I'm sorry, sir, but I can't disclose room numbers like that."

Behind the desk where Claire couldn't see, Marcus released the clasp that held the answer to all the world's problems. He smiled as he reached over and, with two fingers, laid a fifty-dollar bill next to the computer's keyboard.

"It's alright," Marcus said, making sure his voice was significantly detached from her concerns. "I'm an old friend of Roger's." He left the quiet part—*I can get you fired either way you play this*—unsaid.

Claire nervously glanced in either direction as she palmed the money, returning a smiling gaze to Marcus as she began typing on the keyboard. "Is that K-E-E-N?"

"With an E at the end," Marcus said, impressed with the woman's composure.

"Hm," she said, now frowning. "I don't have anyone checked in under that name." She spelled his name out again to confirm, but Marcus' mind was elsewhere.

The bastard lied to me, he thought furiously. But even before he finished that musing, the logic just wasn't there. What good would it do to lure Marcus to the lodge? What possible purpose could it serve a greedy, desperate man like Jonathan?

Claire's voice pierced his circling thoughts. "Do you suppose he made the reservation under a different name?"

Of course. Marcus wanted to laugh. The reason Roger didn't know their old friend was staying at his hotel was because, of course, Jonathan wouldn't use his own name. But what alias...?

An echo from the past trailed Claire's words and a vision appeared between the two of them that only Marcus perceived: the visage of a young man whose face was shadowed by a dark hood. Jonathan's young phantom spoke the name in unison with Marcus.

"Jack Remains."

Claire giggled. "Oh, yeah. I remember him. He checked in on Friday. I thought his name was very strange and he said it was a nickname from where he grew up."

Marcus' vision became distant, looking into the past. He watched sixteen-year-old Jonathan Keene signing his name onto the covenant. "Jack Shit Remains," he said with a scoff, making a show of putting a period after the signature. "That's when I'm coming back, Vandrel. When jack shit remains of your little club."

Claire typed something into the computer—her own digital John Hancock—and then looked back at Marcus with a smile. "He's on the second floor. Room 219."

Not even bothering to smile or thank her, Marcus spun on his heels and walked toward the stairs, eager to be free of the ghost haunting that desk.

Gaining some distance from the lobby, Marcus rekindled his anger over the present situation. He had been biding his time these past twenty years, doing something that went against every aspect of his nature: waiting. He had been waiting for the right time to come again, and after years of careful planning, the stars were finally aligning.

Then here comes old Jack Shit Remains.

Marcus pushed open the door to the stairs and then took them two at a time. His anger was intensifying with every upward lunge.

Of all the members that entered his order, Jonathan Keene was the only one to leave Ransom Creek. It seemed appropriate that the man would return under such ominous circumstances.

Opening the door to the second floor, Marcus was greeted by a maid's cart outside a vacant room. The housekeeper turned to look at him. She looked close to his age, nearing forty or just past, but she seemed almost too elegant to be turning the sheets in the Brookridge.

Marcus nodded toward her as he turned away and strode down the hall toward Jonathan's room. Each step he took down that hall felt like a step back in time, a year at a time. He remembered the last night he came to this place. Marcus had walked these halls just hours before Caroline Kraft would be strangled to death in the ravine, her breathing restricted by a power she couldn't even comprehend.

There were six of them then: himself, Roger, Patrick, Debbie, Jonathan, and Caroline. But was Caroline ever truly one of them? He had spent the years since her death trying to forget what happened in the depths of the Duprees' lodge only to be drawn back here now when he was so close to reclaiming his family's lost legacy.

Every step he took toward Room 219 increased his rage, and by the time he stood before the door he had worked himself into a state of mind that he supposed murderers fell victim to.

Marcus took a deep breath before raising his hand to knock. As he exhaled, the ghosts of the past seemed to release their hold on him, and he rapped on the door almost gently.

There was no answer.

He knocked again, harder this time.

"I was just going to tell the front desk..."

Marcus turned toward the lovely housekeeper who stood by her cart down the hall.

"He was supposed to check out this morning," she explained, approaching Marcus hesitantly. As she neared, he realized that the woman was even more beautiful than he thought, and her presence restored his calm. "But he never came back last night."

"Last night?"

"Yeah, I was working late and I saw someone come to his room—I assumed his daughter. She looked like my son's age, maybe sixteen or seventeen. Black hair, just like him. They left around nine or ten, but I never saw him come back." She motioned toward the closed door. "His things are all still in there, so I was going to let the front desk know I couldn't clean up yet."

Marcus considered the woman's words as his eyes went from her to Room 219. In a daze, he said, "Thank you, ma'am," and strode past her, quickening his pace toward Roger's office.

"Wait, slow down, Marcus," Roger said, getting up from behind his desk. "You're telling me Jon's back in Ransom?"

Marcus ran a hand through his hair, which was as frail and white as an elderly man's. "I didn't want to tell you," he explained, staring blankly at the carpet pattern in Roger's office; he remembered how it had looked splattered with blood. "He checked in under his Jack Remains pseudonym, the one he always said he'd use to write books."

"I don't understand... You said we'd never have to worry about Jon again—that he'd never dare show his face around here after that whole thing with Patrick."

Shaking his head, Marcus waved a hand to disregard Roger's confusion. "Just get the damn keys, Roger. We need to check the room."

Together they returned to Room 219, ensuring the housekeeper had finished her pass of the hallway. Roger used the master key to unlock the room and swung the door open to reveal a disordered scene.

Jonathan's luggage was halfway packed—a small suitcase with enough clothes for a weekend stay. Marcus ignored the clothes and moved toward the small safe near the closet.

"What the hell was he doing here?" Roger wondered aloud. "Why would he be hiding his visit from us?"

Because he's blackmailing me, you fucking moron, Marcus wanted to scream, but he focused on looking for the manuscript. The hotel room's safe was slightly ajar, and when Marcus opened it completely he saw two leather portfolios. He frantically grabbed them, throwing open the first.

"What are you looking for?" Roger asked.

Ignoring the question, Marcus tore the first page of the manuscript out. It read: *The Life of Gustave Moreau* by Jonathan Keene. He stuffed the page back into its home, knowing exactly what *that* book would be about—Jonathan had fancied himself a musician and was fascinated by the superstitions surrounding the French-American composer that gained notoriety in the 1700s for his wife's murder spree.

"Marcus?"

Roger's voice was just a distant whisper to Marcus as he tossed the first portfolio aside and flipped open the next one's flap. The title page inside revealed its contents to be a collection of short stories.

He wouldn't put our story in there, Marcus thought, jamming the page back into the leather satchel and tossing it aside. *He wouldn't bury it.*

"Can you talk to me, Marcus?" Roger was almost shouting now, and if Marcus kept ignoring him the man would certainly make a scene.

"We need to call the police," Marcus instructed as calmly as he could.

Roger recoiled. "You mean Pat?"

"No!" Marcus replied, more sharply than he intended. "Close the door, Roger. We need to talk." When the room was secure, Marcus took a seat on the bed, shoving Jonathan's luggage to the floor. "I don't want Patrick to know what's going on."

Roger crossed his arms. "Can you at least tell me?"

Feeling cornered, Marcus sighed. "Five days ago, Jonathan called me. His publisher has been pressing him for new books—one of which is about what happened..." He looked up into Roger's narrowed eyes. "Downstairs."

Those narrowed eyes widened. So much so that Marcus wondered if Roger had even thought about that night in the twenty years since. It wouldn't come as a shock to him, since Roger never struck him as a man skilled in introspection.

Roger's eyes went from Marcus to the discarded portfolios, then back to Marcus. "He wrote a goddamn book about—" The rest of the sentence was lost as the man's throat seemed to seize up at the prospect of talking about the Caroline Kraft incident.

"So he says," Marcus replied. He motioned toward the safe. "If these were left behind and the safe wasn't secured, I can only assume he took the draft with him so he could properly blackmail me."

A grim silence fell, broken only by Roger's heavy breathing as he slowly pieced together what was happening.

"We need to find him," he said, moving toward the door.

Marcus got up. "You need to call this in—to the police department, not the sheriff's office. Say one of your guests tried to skip their bill, but he's a public figure and it needs to be handled discreetly. We don't want this getting back to Larson. I just don't know if we can trust him to play this cool."

Roger turned. "Why the hell not?! Don't you have Larson under your thumb? What good is owning this town if you don't put them to work for you?!"

"You know why," Marcus growled, feeling his brow tighten to the point of discomfort. "Patrick doesn't know what really happened, and that's likely the only reason he's stayed the course. If he—hell, if anyone reads that book, it's all over."

Slowing his breathing, Roger ran his hands over his balding head, his white dress shirt drenched at the armpits. "Okay, I'll call the chief directly and have him put Don Avery on this. I'll say he stole another guest's confidential files—some kind of boring government contract that'll keep anyone from poking their nose in it. I need to find out when he left…"

"Last night," Marcus replied absently, his vision going distant as he re-called the housekeeper's report. He pictured a teenage girl with jet-black hair accompanying a Jonathan Keene that was now pushing forty. "Your housekeeper… She checked his room this morning…"

"Betsy?"

Marcus snapped his attention back on Roger. "What?"

"Betsy Weathers," Roger said, as if it were obvious. "That's her name."

Everything finally hit Marcus. "I don't care what your fucking maid's name is, Roger! She saw him last night with a teenage girl! It had to be her!" He strode quickly past Roger toward the door.

"Who?!"

Feeling his heart thundering with the sudden revelation, Marcus spun toward his accomplice in a twenty-year-old unsolved murder and with a snarl said, "Caroline."

CHAPTER 4
MISSING REMAINS

"This is not going to work, Chief," Donald explained, tempering his rage as best he could. "I can already tell. The guy has no regard for procedure."

Owen Burke shuffled a stack of papers back into a folder on his desk. "Make it work, Don," he told his senior detective, not even having the balls to look him in the eye. "Sheriff Larson didn't want an outsider to replace Anne either, but not even he could stonewall this. So make it work."

"How did this even get pushed through?" Donald asked, turning in his seat to observe his new partner rocking childishly in Anne's old desk chair out in the bullpen. "Aren't I supposed to have some kind of say? I'm the senior detective now, right?"

The chief's phone rang. "You are the senior detective, Don, which means you have to start doing what I do every day: You have to eat shit and produce results." He picked up the phone. "Yeah? Who? The journalist? Alright... Got it, I'll send 'em over." He hung up. "Call your boy in, Avery."

Donald hesitated, hoping to discuss this matter further. But in that brief silence, Chief Burke gave him that look that said, *Please don't make me pull rank, Avery.*

Reluctantly, Donald got up and pulled the chief's door open. "Rane. Get in here."

Eddie Rane made a show of jogging across the bullpen, sliding past Donald as if he were about to hit him. "Don't run me over again, boss."

Chief Burke snapped his fingers. "Take a seat, Rane."

Both detectives did.

"I understand you got your nose set on Tori Kraft's kid," the chief began, nodding toward the lobby through his office window. "Since you're new here, let me assure you, the daughter will show up. They just moved here over the summer, but there have already been three prior reports of the girl going missing, and each time she showed up a few days later—probably just staying out doing stupid teenage shit in the woods." He presented two upward palms. "Nothing to worry about. The mother took it up with the sheriff and it's not our job to butt in on their cases—they give us the same respect."

Donald thought Eddie was about to interject, but the chief kept going.

"Besides, your first big case just came in. I need you two over at the Brookridge." He turned toward Donald now. "Roger Dupree says someone tried to stiff their bill. Go over there and take his statement."

Leaning forward, Donald said, "With all due respect, sir, why do you need us for that? Shouldn't a patrol officer handle it?"

"Yeah," Eddie added, "or a collection agency. We got a missing girl to find."

Donald clenched his fists, annoyed that this guy was trying to help argue in his favor by using the Kraft girl's situation. He couldn't help thinking of his own daughter, and he momentarily wondered if the frustration he was feeling that morning had more to do with Madison's peer going missing than it had to do with his new partner.

No, he thought, eyeing Eddie picking his teeth from the corner of his vision. *This guy is frustrating enough on his own.*

"This is delicate," Chief Burke explained. "The suspect is a former resident and now a public figure. Jonathan Keene of *The Boston Globe*. You may have read one of his riveting nonfiction books."

The name sounded familiar to Donald, but he only read the local paper and had fallen behind on his nonfiction reading.

"Anyway, you two are handling this because it needs to be kept quiet. Keene's got a bit of a profile and we don't want this getting out. Close it quick. And," Burke continued, pointing a finger at Rane, "you actually *don't* have a missing girl to find, Detective. What you do have is this case that's been assigned to you—your *first* case in my department, Rane, so I suggest you hop to it." He flicked his eyes toward Donald. "This won't be a problem, will it?"

"Sir, no, sir," Eddie said with a salute. He whipped his hand to give Donald's shoulder a light tap as he stood up. "Let's roll, partner."

After Eddie was out of the office, Donald gave it one more desperate attempt. "Please, Chief..."

The man had the decency to at least give a sympathetic look as he said, "It's from above, Detective. Eat shit. Get results."

"Seems like you got it made here, man."

Donald gave Eddie a sidelong look, not wanting to engage but also not wanting to suffer whatever results he'd face for not giving the man the attention he craved. "Is that right?"

Eddie motioned out the window as they drove down Parkview in Donald's car. "Sleepy town. Sleepier chief. Can't imagine you have a lot of bank robberies here, right? I'd be shocked if your tactical guys even had to raid a drug den." He laughed. "And here we are, chasing down a city slicker who skipped the bill at the local lodge. High stakes, baby!"

"Sounds like you miss Charlotte," Donald said, turning down State Street. "What brought you to Ransom?"

"Long story," Eddie said, keeping his eyes on the passing storefronts of downtown. "I have a feeling you probably know as much as you should know about the situation, so it's probably not my place to elaborate."

"Actually," Donald replied, "I know nothing about why you're here. Seems kind of sudden."

Eddie drummed his fingers on the passenger door before replying with a simple, "Yep."

They went the next two blocks without saying anything, for which Donald was thankful. But then Eddie turned to him and asked, "This your first divorce?"

Sudden anger made Donald almost swerve out of the lane, but he composed himself as he glared at his nosy partner. Eddie just nodded to the envelope that was now tucked between Donald's seat and the car's middle console.

"I've gotten two of those," Eddie said with a smirk. "Both times were a relief, so if you want to go out for celebratory drinks later, I'm buying."

"No thanks," Donald said coldly, turning his attention back to the road. He didn't want to give Rane the satisfaction of seeing him riled.

They drove the rest of the way to Brookridge in silence.

Eddie whistled as they stepped into the Brookridge Lodge. "Jesus, this place is nuts."

Donald adjusted his jacket, sparing a glance at Eddie's unprofessional attire. He felt embarrassed to be on a case with someone who looked like they just got out of a Pearl Jam concert. But the chief's words kept echoing in his mind.

Just eat shit, Don, he told himself. *Focus on the job.*

"Detective Avery."

Roger Dupree was waiting for them as they crossed the lobby, and Donald made sure he was a step ahead of his partner so he could put the department's best foot forward. "Hey, Roger. Heard you had a little trouble this morning."

"You could say that," Roger said with what Donald thought was a nervous laugh.

Why's he seem edgy? Donald wondered, knowing the man to normally be a collected, albeit boring, businessman. Would a guest sneaking out without paying really rattle him?

"Someone empty the minibar and bail after they saw the tab?" Eddie asked.

Roger tilted his head, looked at Donald, and then extended his hand toward Eddie. "I don't believe we've met, Detective. Roger Dupree. Owner and operator of the Brookridge Lodge."

Eddie shook his hand firmly. "Detective Eddie Rane. Nice to meet you. Why don't you show us the great disappearing journalist's room."

Donald gave Roger a slight nod, excusing Eddie's tact.

"Right this way."

As they made their way upstairs, Roger filled them in on the situation. "You might have heard of Jon Keene," he told Donald. "Writes for *The Globe* now, but he used to report for *The Courier* downtown back when you were probably still in high school. Anyway, I suspect he's had a hard time of it lately because we had several complaints that he had been badgering guests, grilling them for anything that might make a good story—must need something to sell." He lowered his voice as they got off the elevator on the second floor. "We even had a guest who works for the government say he took one of her contracts—so if you happen to find that, please, for both our sakes, keep it sealed and let us get it back to her. She said it might be in a leather portfolio."

"Sure," Donald said. "That guest still here? We'd like to talk to her, especially if she interacted with Keene at all."

Even though Donald couldn't see Roger's face, he could tell from the man's hesitation that the request was unwelcome.

"I'll check with the front desk on that," he finally replied. "Up here is Jon's room. We left it as we found it."

"You knew Keene, right?" Eddie asked. "I understand you're a lifelong resident, and it sounds like you may have crossed paths with a famous journalist originally from here."

Roger stopped in front of Room 219 and faced the detectives. Donald noticed his features looked more relaxed now, as if he had been waiting for the question. "Yeah, we went to high school together," Roger said. "Even hung out at some of the same parties. But I wouldn't say we were close enough that he'd bother giving me a ring when coming to town."

Eddie leaned against the wall and crossed his arms. "Not even when he stays at your hotel? I assume he knew you took over the place for your dad back in '87."

Donald discreetly gave Eddie a sidelong look, wondering how he seemed to already know so much about Ransom Creek.

Shrugging, Roger just motioned toward the door. "I'd love to ask him about it. Maybe if you guys can find him, we'll see what he has to say." Roger looked down either end of the hall before leaning toward the detectives. "Speaking of which: Jon used an alias when he checked in. So it seems he had no interest in catching up with me."

"Alias?" Donald pulled his notebook from his jacket's inside pocket.

Roger chuckled. "It was some dumb joke back in the day. He had this saying about getting out of this town—something about that 'Jack & Diane' Mellencamp song. I think he wrote an editorial about it one time in *The Courier*." Donald noticed that Roger's eyes became distant for a moment before he looked back at them. "Jack Remains. Something about 'only Jack remains where he was born' or 'Jack remains where he'll die,' I don't remember. You can probably look it up. But I gave my staff an earful for not looking into such a bizarre name given by a guest."

Donald jotted the name down and flipped his notebook shut. "You mind unlocking the door? Just give us a few minutes to look around and we can come back to your office to finish talking."

"Sure thing." Roger produced the key and let them in. "Just give me a shout if you need anything. Like I said, we found the room like this—no luggage or anything. Sorry there's not much really to go off of."

After Roger was gone, Eddie closed the door to the room. "I'm guessing you know he's lying."

Of course Donald knew he was lying about something, but he didn't really like how Rane was acting like he already had this entire town and its residents figured out. "Roger's always watching out for this place's reputation. Could just be him not wanting anything nefarious being associated with his business."

Eddie opened the bathroom door and peered in. "Could be our missing hack was putting together a hit piece on this place. Roger certainly wouldn't want that getting out. Maybe called the Ransom Creek mob and strapped a pair of cement shoes to Johnny and pushed him into—"

"Let's focus on the facts," Donald interrupted, kneeling down to inspect the room's safe. It looked unused.

"They didn't find the place like this," Eddie said, motioning to the one bed in the room. "You ever stay in a hotel room and leave a bed like that? That's not slept-in messy—that's staged messy. Somebody wanted it to look used."

Donald stood up and regarded the sheets. Eddie was right. The bed looked intentionally ruffled, as if someone had made the bed and then quickly unmade it.

"Also," Eddie wondered aloud, pacing the length of the bed as he pulled back his green jacket sleeve to read his watch, "it's 9 a.m. on a Monday morning. Seems weird to be calling the cops in on a skipped bill so urgently, right?"

"Agreed," Donald said, if a little reluctantly. Eddie was abrasive, but he might not be a bad investigator. For some reason that annoyed Donald, as if he craved his own preemptive judgment of Eddie to be confirmed. Regardless, he pulled out his notebook and wrote *bed*, *time*, and *who else in room?*

As if he could see what Donald wrote, Eddie asked, "Who all do you think had access to the room before Roger was alerted? We have to assume housekeeping."

Donald pictured Madison's friend Elijah's mom, Betsy; a cute single mother who lived in the same trailer park as Tori Kraft. That correlation tried desperately to board Donald's train of thought, but those tracks were already laid and he left the detail behind for now as Eddie kept talking.

"Even if Keene asked for an early checkout, they wouldn't need to turn down the room right away. Someone was definitely looking for this guy before we were called in. I think we need to put the screws to Dupree, partner."

Donald tucked his notepad back into his jacket as he spun on Eddie. "Put the screws to him? Look, we're not in a movie, Rane. I don't know if you're looking for big city action here, but we're not going to sweat local business owners who call us in for help."

"Come on," Eddie said, his voice thick with doubtful mirth. "You don't buy this. I know small towns like this tend to sweep things under the rug, but—"

"We're not sweeping anything under the rug," Donald said, more forcefully than intended. But Eddie seemed determined to push all his buttons on the worst morning of his life. The divorce was still weighing on him, and the thought of Betsy Weathers reminded him of his awkward breakfast with Madison. Dealing with a Martin Riggs wannabe was the last thing he needed. "We're following procedure. Us small-town folk like to keep our community in order, and that means following some goddamn standards."

Eddie nodded with a smile. He uncrossed his arms and put his hands in his pockets as he stepped toward Donald. "You know, back in Charlotte, I had a partner like you. Marty O'Donnell. Retired in '92. Solid dude, always had my back. But he had this tendency to weigh every decision during a case against the chief's image. Guy would do anything, so long as the boss said it was the right thing to do."

Donald waited for the punchline.

"Thing is," Eddie continued, with an expression on his face that Donald could only perceive as condescending, "our chief was skimming from the evidence locker—had one too many vices, ya know? When the IA came sniffing in '93, old Chief Roberts hung O'Donnell out to dry. All the evidence was there, because Marty always played by the chief's rules. They rescinded his retirement—for which he got a shiny gold watch after nearly twenty-five years of service—and gave him a seven-year sentence instead." Eddie's smile faded as he pointed over his shoulder. "You can see O'Donnell upstate, still singing the same song—insisting he was just following orders."

Letting the silence hang for a moment, Donald ran his tongue over his lower teeth. "Let's go chat with Betsy. Then I'll take the lead on Dupree. Understood?"

Eddie stepped aside and made a grand gesture to let Donald pass.

They found Betsy Weathers restocking her cart on the lower floor. Not wanting to alert Roger that they'd be questioning his staff, they avoided asking the front desk for Betsy's whereabouts and instead just roamed the halls until they happened upon her.

Betsy heard them coming and finished putting two bottles of glass cleaner on the lower rack of her cart. She straightened and pushed the two strands of hair on either side of her head behind her ears.

"Morning, Betsy," Donald said, resting his hands on his hips so that she could see his badge. Everyone in town knew him to be a detective, but it didn't hurt to establish his presence here as an officer of the law and not just Madison Avery's father. "Could we ask you about the situation with Room 219?"

She looked from Donald to Eddie, whose presence seemed to almost overwhelm her.

"Oh," Donald said, motioning to his partner. "This is Detective Eddie Rane. My big-city replacement."

Eddie snorted a laugh. "Everyone here acts like Charlotte is New York or something. Pleasure to meet you, Mrs. Weathers."

"It's Betsy," she said shyly. "And Charlotte's lovely. I haven't been in years, but I love that city. What part are you from?"

Jesus, Donald thought, *is she flirting with this guy?*

"South End, mostly," Eddie replied. "Used to be able to hear the breweries warming up before noon. Honestly thought I'd live and die at Sycamore until winding up here."

Betsy smiled at that and may have kept chatting, but Donald plowed ahead.

"Were you making the rounds early this morning?"

She looked abashed as she nodded her head. "I was out sick yesterday morning, so some of the rooms didn't get turned—all our summer help is gone, and it's just me on the weekends."

Sick, Donald thought. *You mean strung out.* Betsy Weathers was a recovering groupie, having made the rounds with all the big hair metal bands in the 80s. There wasn't a huge drug scene in Ransom Creek, but

Donald knew Betsy was tapped into it. Her son, Elijah, had already been caught with weed twice that spring.

"Anyway," Betsy said, motioning to the cart, "I worked overnight to catch up—Roger let me shift my hours as long as I was able to finish the second floor. That's when I saw that Jack or whatever his name was sneaking off with—well." Her gaze had been wandering, but now she focused on the detectives. "I thought it might have been his daughter or something, because she didn't look much older than Elijah. But maybe it was...something else? You know?"

Donald gave Eddie another of his sidelong looks.

"Given the hour," Betsy added, "they didn't seem to want to be seen or heard. I was around the corner near the elevators, so I didn't get a great look. And they didn't see me."

"Could you describe the girl?" Eddie asked.

Donald listened carefully as Betsy Weathers described someone that much too closely fit the description of their other missing person, Rachel Kraft.

CHAPTER 5
THE GROWING SHADOW

O utside the lodge, Eddie paced while Donald scribbled in his notepad on the roof of his car.

"I still think we should corner Dupree on this. You saw how that babe clammed up when you asked about the room. There's no way she wouldn't have at least peeked in there before going to the boss."

"No reason to lay this out for Roger yet," Donald said, jotting down a reminder to get an official statement from Betsy. "We have some angles to chase. I think we start with Rachel Kraft."

Eddie stopped pacing and Donald could feel the look of disbelief. But instead of waiting for the wisecrack, he snapped his notebook shut and turned to face him.

"Let's grab a bite and then head to the high school."

To Eddie's credit, he didn't gloat about the strange circumstances of the morning guiding them back to the missing girl. For that much, at least, Donald was grateful.

The way his morning had gone, he'd take just about any glimmer of hope.

"So who's this Vandrel guy?"

Donald looked at the passing billboard that Eddie motioned toward. Emerging from the trees, it was a big red sign with the Vandrel Group's real estate company logo emblazoned on it. "Local philanthropist," Donald replied.

"Bright Hollow. Affordable living, priceless peace of mind," Eddie read aloud in a mock TV commercial voice. "Let me guess: trailer park?"

Despite his dour mood, Donald allowed himself a chuckle. "Bingo. Town council made a stink about the place going up a couple years ago, thinking it would bring in the wrong crowd. But our very own Betsy Weathers shacked up there when her house foreclosed."

"That rock n' roll lifestyle can be hard to shake," Eddie said, tapping out a rhythm on the passenger door. "Glad I hung it up when I did."

Donald gave another half-hearted laugh. "Had you pinned as a rock star. Let me guess: you were the frontman?" *Center of attention,* he thought.

"Drummer," Eddie said absently, staring into the passing trees as if they reminded him of his lost youth. "My brother was the singer. Before he died."

Any levity Donald allowed himself completely deflated at that moment. Detective Edward Rane's humanity hit him like a mule kick to his gut. "Sorry," he managed.

"Nah," Eddie said, tapping his fingers again. "It was his choice—his terms. But, made it so I never wanted to play music again." He gave a morbid laugh. "Guess the son of a bitch did us both a favor. Otherwise, I'd be stuck in Bright Hollow, maybe delivering pizzas between gigs, and you'd have a much more boring partner to deal with."

If only, Donald thought as he turned into the diner. He noticed in the rearview mirror he was smiling.

Elijah Weathers nearly fell on his ass while trying to descend the incline. He avoided the hiking paths and the cool staircase that gave parkgoers easy access to the lower ravine. Too many eyes, even on a Monday. His dealer, Molly, got easily spooked.

Sliding on dried leaves and other woodland debris, he finally managed to reach the rock-strewn footing where the creek was most shallow. He could follow that the rest of the way to his meeting place.

Brushing the ravine's leavings off his baggy pants, he quickened his pace so he could get back to school before lunch was over. He was freaking starving. Also, he was in a hurry to be done with this exchange. Molly wasn't the most pleasant person in the world, and the last few Mondays she had hinted at raising the price.

"Y'all are smoking me dry," she had complained last time. "I think you should start selling for me. Those rich kids you hang out with should be footing the bill a little, yeah?"

Elijah had sidestepped that suggestion, not wanting to tell her that weed was really all he had to offer. Without it, what was he? Just a trailer trash kid trapped in an Eddie Bauer catalog: no prospects and nothing to use as a social bargaining chip.

What he did have was balls. Neither Jared nor Cliff had the sacks to meet drug dealers or stash narcotics in their house. And neither of them had a mom that was too busy trying to score at the bar to worry about what her son was up to.

So, Eli did everything he could to hang onto his status as the good times supplier, hoping that no one with bigger balls—or maybe just less to lose—threatened his place.

He found Molly sitting on the huge rock near the creek's bend. As usual, she had her nose in a thick fantasy novel, but when she heard Eli coming she pushed her considerable form to her feet.

"I could smell you coming down the hill," she said, waving a hand in front of her face. "That's some mad gas you got there."

"What?" Eli said with a laugh, and he thought he also caught a whiff of something. But when he sniffed again, it was just the usual damp smell of the ravine.

She just nodded toward him, lowering her sunglasses slightly. "You bring a little extra this time? Like we talked about?"

Eli did, but he wasn't willing to part with it yet. "I think I'll be fine with a dub again. Football's starting back up, so I don't think Jared will be partaking as often. It'll probably just be me and Cliff. Maybe Maddie since her parents are splitting up."

Molly pushed her glasses back up and made that face: tight mouth, puffed-out cheeks. He felt guilty for thinking she looked kind of like a pig in disguise. Then she let out a breath that flapped her lips. "Fine, but I need you to step it up here. This drive sucks, and gas ain't gettin' any cheaper, budmeister."

Eli sighed as he nodded, and again he thought he smelled something foul. Did Molly blow ass and try to blame it on him?

She snapped her fingers and motioned for Eli to pony up his dough. He reached into his front pocket, making sure to only grab one of the two twenties he had for lunch over the next couple of weeks. His mom didn't keep their fridge stocked, but she did manage to provide him a steady food allowance that he mostly spent on the one thing that might keep him from being a total social outcast.

Molly took the bill between two fingers and tried to look smooth by producing a rolled-up baggie from her jacket pocket with her other hand. "Seriously, dog," she said again. "You having stomach issues or something?"

Eli looked around, sniffing again. "No, I smell that too. Maybe an animal took a shit nearby?"

She made a puking sound. "Fuckin' nasty-ass animal if so." But she began sniffing again, walking toward the tree line. "Think it's coming from over here."

Out of pure curiosity, Eli followed her. The smell got much stronger as he followed her into the copse that had screened their view into the ravine.

Molly gasped. "Dude... Holy shit!"

Eli pushed a branch out of his face as he moved beside Molly. Despite the thick smell, he breathed in a deep, shocked breath as well.

While Eli loved scary movies, and had seen tons of brutal deaths on screen, he had never seen an actual dead body like this before. An old white guy with a receding hairline and a leather satchel tucked under his arm lay sprawled in the crushed leaves.

The man's eyes were wide, staring upward in a mask of eternal fear—as if he had been watching his death descend from the sky like a dark-winged nightmare. While one arm cradled the case under it like a top secret file, the dead man's other hand gripped a piece of paper splattered with blood.

His neck was...wrong. It looked longer than it should, like someone tried to rip it off, and bruise-colored smears streaked across the skin. Elijah pictured a huge monster with ashen hands wringing the poor dude's neck.

"What the fuck?" Molly said, her voice still devoid of logic or understanding. "Dude's dead..."

Eli had no response. His body was an icy statue that wanted to tremble but couldn't. The only part of him that moved were his eyes, which went from the crumpled paper to the dark bruises on the man's neck, just above his ripped collar; violet fingers had strangled him and left their stain.

His eyes went back to the paper, and even though it was crushed and splattered, he saw the neatly typed words near the bottom of the page:

Wasn't there supposed to be a bonfire?

A wolf howled in the distance and Eli screamed.

Eddie yawned as he poured himself more coffee. "I take it you got some kids?"

He saw Donald finally look up from his notepad, that same look on his face as when Eddie had brought up the divorce.

"Seeing how you knew the Kraft girl, I'm guessing you got a kid who's a classmate."

Donald didn't answer, but the way he went back to his notes told Eddie his hunch was right. "I also never met a guy going through a divorce who wasn't a little relieved...unless they had kids." He took a sip of his coffee. "When my parents split up, my dad never wanted to talk about it either. Went to his grave without ever talking about it."

"Let's just focus on the case," Donald said, flipping back through his notes.

The waitress set down their lunch. A ham and swiss for Eddie and tuna melt for Donald.

"Thanks," Eddie said to the woman, who had already moved to the booth behind them. He leaned over his plate and grabbed a chip. "I think better when I'm not thinking about work," he said before taking a bite. "Tell me about your kid."

Donald flipped another page in his notebook, but Eddie suspected he wasn't even interested in the contents. "I actually think better when I am thinking about work, so..."

"I'm guessing they're a straight-A student, yeah? Quarterback? Or captain of the cheerleading squad?"

Closing his notebook, Donald finally looked up. "My daughter is a senior at Valley High. I don't know how close she is with Tori's daughter, since the Krafts just moved into Bright Hollow over the summer."

Eddie took a bite of his toasted sandwich, chewing while he said, "So our missing girl was the new kid in town. Same grade as yours?"

Donald nodded as he took a bite of his own lunch. He kept his mouth closed while chewing.

"That means little Rachel was probably an outcast. If your daughter *is* close with her, there's a very good chance she'll know where she is, but it also means she likely won't tell you."

After swallowing, Donald asked why he thought that.

Eddie set his sandwich down and grabbed his coffee again. "New kid comes in at the tail end of high school, living in the trailer park, sees all these kids living in this Hallmark ad of a town—their nice houses, clean streets." He gulped the rest of his coffee and added, "That's a recipe for a runaway, and those don't usually vanish cleanly unless someone's scrubbing the tracks."

Donald didn't reply immediately; his eyes shifted toward the window, and Eddie could tell something just came to him.

"What you got?"

Donald's attention returned, but he didn't get a chance to reply; once his mouth opened, his pager went off.

"That's dispatch," he said, grabbing his wallet from his jacket pocket and dropping a twenty.

Eddie shoved the remaining half of his sandwich in his mouth as he followed.

"I told you," he said with a full mouth, pulling his green jacket back on. "Stop thinking about work for a minute—I know you got something..."

Roger's phone startled him. He buckled his pants and tucked the *Playboy* magazine back into his desk drawer. Out of pure habit, he adjusted his tie before picking up the handset.

"Hello?"

Patrick's angered voice was unmistakable. "Did you seriously put the P.D. out to find Jon?"

Roger's chest tightened and all he could get out was, "Huh?"

"He's dead," Patrick hissed, as if he didn't want to be heard. "Someone fucking killed him and dumped him in the ravine! Some trailer trash kid called it in, and apparently the P.D. opened a missing persons case this morning with you as a witness."

Roger tried to speak again, but he could only make a strange croaking sound. His mind was racing.

"Dupree!"

"Yeah!" Roger shouted, startling himself to his feet. "I called it in. Marcus insisted."

There was a short pause before Patrick barked again. "He insisted you report Jon missing to the goddamn P.D.?! Why wouldn't he call me?! What was Keene even doing here?"

"Wait, Pat... Are you saying Jonathan's dead?"

"Get your ass down here, Roger! I want to know what the fuck is going on!"

Before Roger could answer, the line died. As he carefully set the phone back on its base, he wondered if he should call Marcus. The knock on his door nearly gave him a heart attack.

"What?!"

His office door clicked open. "Mr. Dupree?" Claire poked her head in. "I'm sorry to disturb you, but this was left at the front desk—I didn't see who dropped it off..."

Roger stepped around his desk to take the envelope from her before she retreated from his frantic energy.

He held the envelope for a long moment, staring at it, waiting for it to burst into flames. When it didn't, he moved to open it, but paused once more when he saw the blood.

It was a small pimple, almost like a dot from a red ink pen. But when he moved his thumb near it, the gruesome rose bloomed and veined its way into the white paper.

Roger tore it open and read the blood-splattered page inside. It was a gruesome memory he had sealed away in the recesses of his mind—a vivid description of the worst night of his life.

It was the death of Caroline Kraft.

He dropped the page and flexed his fingers to see the blood was on his hands.

CHAPTER 6
BEFORE IT STARTS

E ddie smoothed his mustache as he got out of Donald's car, his gaze fixed on the two sheriff deputies giving him stink-eyes. "Something tells me we're the third nut here, Don." He was still chewing on a toothpick from the diner.

"It's Donald," his partner replied. "Let me handle this."

Donald strode toward the two sheriff cruisers as Eddie took off his sunglasses and observed the crime scene. The woods were yellow-taped just beyond the two tan cruisers blocking the parking lot entrance. Out of the corner of his eye, Eddie caught sight of Sheriff Larson talking to a phenomenally dressed middle-aged man that looked like some British lord with thin white hair.

Now that's gotta be Marcus Vandrel, Eddie thought, remembering the man's billboard from before. Why's a real estate mogul hanging out at a murder scene? Did he own the park or have some claim over the hiking trails? He filed that away for later and joined his partner.

"...well, we were on his case when he was missing," Donald was saying.

"He's certainly been found now," one of the sheriff's men said. His name tag said *Deputy Dougherty*. "And murder falls under county jurisdiction."

"And if the victim is the subject of an ongoing investigation," Eddie interjected, rolling the toothpick to the other side of his mouth, "seems customary to maybe let the assigned officers close out the case before handing it over to the new team. Don't you think?"

Deputy Dougherty gave Eddie a callous look before turning to his own partner, Deputy Armstrong, who looked much more eager for a confrontation. However, after staring Eddie down for a beat, he must have thought better of it; he simply motioned toward the yellow tape.

"Go close it out," Armstrong offered. "We'll give you five minutes to confirm that your man's been found. But stay out of forensics' way."

Donald gave Eddie a look of pure impotent, cowardice—at least from Eddie's point of view—and nodded for him to follow. Taking the toothpick between thumb and finger, Eddie pointed it at Armstrong as he passed. "Don't start the timer. My partner needs a few minutes to stretch out before he bends completely over for you."

Expectedly, Donald Avery didn't get the joke. "Someone died down here, Rane. Show some damn respect."

Ignoring the retort, Eddie glanced back over toward the sheriff to make sure he wasn't watching them breach the crime scene. But Larson was still speaking animatedly with Ransom's version of Hugh Hefner.

What I wouldn't give to read lips, he thought.

They descended the incline without using the stairs, since there might still be footprints. It was slow going, but Eddie secretly hoped the two dopes up the hill tried to time them. He wouldn't mind giving the sheriff another headache after their chat that morning.

"That's him alright," Donald said. "Never met the guy, but seen enough pictures of him."

"Ransom's own Dan Rather, huh?"

Donald pulled out his notebook. "Something like that."

Eddie lowered himself into a catcher's squat, inspecting the bruising on Jonathan's neck. The man's eyes were skyward, as if he had been pinned down and strangled. The neck looked longer than it should, but Eddie would have to let the autopsy decide that.

"Must have been a big boy atop him," Eddie offered. "The way he's positioned here, must have been choked out by someone heavy enough to keep him down."

"Or he had help," Donald offered, pacing slowly around Keene's body. "Couple guys pinned him down while another restricted his airway."

"No luggage." Eddie stood back up, looking up the hill. "No cars up there in the parking lot except for Beavis and Butthead's cruisers. Must have met someone here." He turned back around and motioned to the leather satchel. "Some kind of exchange."

Donald lowered himself to peer into the pouch, its flap only partially closed. "Whatever he brought was taken."

"A book," Eddie said. "I've seen authors and students around campus using those to protect their manuscripts. Kind of like an old-school status thing—I think Hemingway made those popular, right? At least with pretentious writers."

Donald shook his head. "Roger said he took some contract or something from another guest, said it'd be in something like this."

Eddie inclined his head doubtfully. "I'm not buying that unless we hear it from the horse's mouth. Like you said, let's stick to the facts. We have a dead writer with an empty manuscript receptacle, so we work from that."

"So, someone wanted whatever it was Keene was working on," Donald offered, jotting notes in his book. "And he couldn't be bothered to check out of his hotel room, which means this wasn't necessarily a scheduled exchange...or even voluntary."

"Maybe Johnny was working on a hit piece," Eddie thought out loud, only half-invested in the sudden theory. "Whoever the subject was didn't want him publishing it. But..."

Donald looked up at him.

Eddie shook his head slowly. "What about the girl?"

Seeing his partner look back at the body, Eddie could tell Donald was already dismissing Rachel Kraft as a suspect, for which Eddie wouldn't fault him. Despite some of the wild things he had seen in Charlotte, not even he could picture a seventeen-year-old girl doing something like this.

She could have been a witness, Eddie thought.

The detectives looked at each other then, as if they had just come to the same conclusion.

"Detectives."

That conclusion was put on hold as they watched Sheriff Larson carelessly descend the stairs.

"Not worried about footprints?" Eddie asked with as much insolence as he could muster. "Might have been handy to check for some if you want to solve this murder."

Larson ignored that, only having eyes for Donald Avery. "Don't you and your new partner have P.D. work to focus on? I have plenty of men on this."

"Sir," Donald began in a voice so meek that it made Eddie's testicles retreat into his stomach, "this man is a person of interest in a case we're on. We just need a few minutes to—"

"I don't think so, Detectives," Larson interrupted. He hooked a thumb over his shoulder. "I'm going to need you to clear out. Forensics is coming out and they'll have a full report that we'll send your way."

"We won't be in your way," Eddie said, once more without disguising his utter disdain for the man.

"That's right," Larson snapped, taking a step toward Eddie. "You won't be in our way. I believe you have another missing person that needs to be found—this one hopefully still alive, Detective Rane." The sheriff took another step toward Eddie. "Rachel Kraft may not have a senator for a daddy, but maybe you can track her down before she does something stupid as well."

Acid rose in Eddie's stomach as he tried to contain his anger. He knew the sheriff let Tori's report sit for two days, completely ignoring it. But now Larson was tossing it in their faces like it was their fuck-up.

Larson turned back to Avery. "I'd hate to have to take this up with Chief Burke. Seems like you should be setting a better example for your new partner here, Donnie." He turned his back to them. "Now get out of my crime scene, Detectives. Go find that girl."

"Rachel Kraft?"

Like most of the other kids in class, Madison turned to regard the empty desk near the back of class.

The substitute teacher cleared his throat. "No Rachel Kraft?"

"Ding dong, the witch is gone."

The raucous laughter that followed Cody Page's stupid joke surprised Madison. *How old are we?* she wondered, turning back toward the meek little man who was subbing for their normal English teacher, Mrs. Hobbs.

"That's enough now," the sub said, barely audible over the class's mockery. He bent over his attendance sheet and marked Rachel absent.

While the man finished calling off their names, Madison glanced back at the only empty desk in the room. Thinking about that strange encounter with Rachel on Friday night, an eerie chill ran down her neck. She brushed it away, as if it were a bug, and spun back toward the front of the class.

But something caught her eye.

Outside in the hall, Madison saw Eli motioning for her. A curious scene played out in her mind, in which her friend had snuck into class, brushed her neck with his finger to get her attention, and then darted back out into the hall, leaving behind only an animated cloud like in those old cartoons.

Madison looked back at the sub, who was still rattling off names, and then back to Eli. The latter looked panicked, as if he had urgent news to share with her. Her curiosity overpowered her dislike for causing a scene in school and she raised her hand.

"May I please use the restroom?"

The sub's beady eyes peered over his thick-framed glasses, and he thankfully gave her a detached nod. "Yes, Miss Avery, you may."

Out in the hall, Eli motioned for her to follow him toward the east stairwell. She almost had to run to keep up with him.

"Eli, what are you doing?"

But he didn't respond or slow his pace. He disappeared around the corner and Madison jogged to join him. When she rounded the corner, she almost shrieked. Eli's face was mere inches from hers and his expression was wide-eyed panic.

"She killed someone," he whispered, his hands deep in his pockets. He looked like a homeless person digging for their final coin that certainly didn't exist. "I think she—I don't know. She had to have been there."

"Been where?" Madison asked, not sure if she should be taking him seriously. She lowered her voice and leaned closer. "Who are you talking about? Are you high? Or on something?"

Eli's eyes seemed to relax at that. "I wish. I was in the woods meeting Molly. We saw..." He licked his lips, looking over Madison's shoulder. When he met her eyes again, she thought he might be crying. "We saw a dead guy."

Madison's first instinct was to shove him and tell him to stop messing with her. But she held his gaze, and in those terrified eyes, she could see he wasn't joking. He looked truly shaken. This being an actual possibility of her friend coming across a corpse, her first thoughts went to her father.

"Did you call the police?!"

He nodded. "Yeah, but...I didn't stay. The sheriff came before the cops and Molly split. They basically told me to get lost."

"Okay," Madison said, not really sure what else she could say. Was she supposed to comfort him? This wasn't the type of situation she was prepared for, and none of the teen movies she saw really covered this stuff. Her racing mind went back to what he had started with.

"What did you mean *she* killed someone? Are you talking about Molly?"

Eli shook his head. He finally drew his left hand out of his pocket, revealing a folded-up piece of paper flecked with blood. It shook in his hand as he held it out to her.

Madison didn't want to take it; knew that she shouldn't. It was like her rational mind was overpowered by a dark curiosity which begged to know what answers that paper held. Her fingerprints would tie her fate with Eli's, but Madison didn't allow logic to find its footing.

Grabbing the bloody paper, she unfolded it and read the neatly typed words.

Bonfires were a Ransom Creek ritual up until that night. But rarely were they held that deep in the ravine.

Too many roots underfoot. Too much canopy overhead. And yet, the smoke was there that night. I remember it, thin and bluish, curling through the trees like a serpent caught between worlds. The kids of Ransom Creek weren't supposed to party down there, but in 1974, there were no rules—not for them. Not when you were born on the right side of the creek. Not when your father sat on the council.

Caroline Kraft wasn't supposed to be there—I know that now. Marcus was wrong about her; she wasn't Walter's chosen.

But she came. Barefoot, even, just as Debbie instructed. Black hair down to her waist and eyes like storm glass. The girl who lived in the cursed manor—said to have killed her own father after fucking him, if you believe all the stories. She said things that summer no one wanted to hear. Said the shadows in the creek could talk if you listened. Said Adratheon had called her, but she couldn't have known that name...

Marcus told us the Krafts were servants of a god they couldn't name. But she knew his name, I said.

When we began chanting, I could see Patrick hesitate—he knew something was wrong before Marcus, and not even I fully understood what we had done until it was too late.

They said it was an accident.

They said she fell.

They said she was high.

But before those black hands rose, I swear I heard her whisper something to Roger. I was too far to hear clearly, but later—when the nightmares came, and I had to relive it almost every night since—I knew.

She just wanted to be one of us. Almost every night I hear her ghost ask: "Wasn't there supposed to be a bonfire?"

Madison heard Rachel Kraft say that last part, an echo from the moment before the girl's disappearance on Friday.

And now she isn't in school, Madison thought.

The intercom startled them both, and Madison crumpled the paper up and jammed it into her own pocket.

"Madison Avery, please report to the principal's office immediately. Madison Avery, to the principal's office."

CHAPTER 7
WITCHCRAFT

E ddie paced the principal's office while he waited for the man to return. Donald had left to speak with his daughter, so round one with Principal Vickers was going to be unsupervised, which certainly sat well with Eddie.

The office had wood paneling, which reminded Eddie of his own high school back in Toledo, Ohio. There were dozens of framed photos and plaques on the wall, recounting a storied career as an educator for old Barry Vickers.

Eddie's eyes were drawn to a symmetrical arrangement of smaller photos that were dated all the way back to 1958. Each photo captured the senior class of a given school year. However, there was a gap. The *Class of 1973* was hung right next to *Class of 1975*.

It seemed relatively innocuous, but that didn't stop Eddie from pulling out his notebook. He cracked it open—it opened like a little leatherbound novel, it didn't flip open easily like the ones most cops carried—and wrote down the missing school year.

When the door clicked open, Eddie closed his book, crossed his arms in a show of casual detachment, and turned to face the boss of Valley High.

"Sorry to keep you waiting, Detective," he said.

"You're fine," Eddie replied kindly. "Was just admiring your long career here."

"Yes," Barry said, stopping in front of the wall of pictures on his way to his desk. With his hands in his suit pockets, the principal looked like how Eddie envisioned Donald Avery looking in a few decades. "It makes me feel young or old, depending on the day," he laughed. He was a handsome man, still in decent shape for someone who had to be close to seventy. A silver fox, some might call him.

There was something about him that unsettled Eddie, but it might have just been good old-fashioned jealousy. He could only hope he aged that well.

Eddie took a seat in front of the desk while Barry eased himself in behind it.

"What can I do for you today?"

"I was wondering if you might be able to tell me about one of your seniors," Eddie began, tapping his pen against the cover of his notebook. "Rachel Kraft. Just started here this fall."

"Yes," Vickers said immediately, as if he was either accustomed to the police asking about her or had otherwise expected it. "I actually spoke to the sheriff this weekend about her."

Eddie stopped tapping his pen, taking a steady breath before asking, "What about?" He reopened the notebook even though he already doubted Vickers would give him anything to write down.

The principal coughed slightly, clearly buying himself time to consider his response. "Well, uh, Sheriff Larson said her mother reported her missing again. I assume she's since been found?"

Kind of hard to be found when no one's looking for you, Eddie thought, but instead he just shook his head.

Vickers straightened in his chair. "Oh. I'm sorry, she's just... Well, I'm sure you know it's not the first time her mother has reported her missing."

"Right," Eddie said, giving the man his phoniest smile possible. "And I'm sure it's not the first time the sheriff has put forth his best effort in finding her."

The principal didn't seem to know what to make of that, but Eddie pushed forward.

"What can you tell me about Rachel's time here at your school? I'll go out on a limb and say she's probably not prom queen material, am I right?" His laugh was meant to draw out any venom the principal might have, but his reaction told Eddie there wasn't much in the man.

"Well, it's quite tricky coming into a new school," he replied with a tight smile. "Especially her senior year." His eyes moved toward the wall then. "And, given her family..."

Eddie held his gaze on Vickers. "What about her family?" He pictured her hot mom, and something about the way the man was talking about her didn't sit well with him.

"I guess you're new here as well," Barry said distantly, still staring at the pictures on the wall. "You don't know about the Krafts..."

"Dad?" Madison stepped into the conference room and let the heavy door close behind her. "What's wrong?"

Donald could tell she knew something already; he was well studied on behavioral patterns associated with lying. But he wasn't prepared to push her yet. Given the morning's events, he wasn't feeling particularly confrontational. Instead, he just gave her a tight smile and motioned to one of the empty seats.

"I wanted to talk to you before you start hearing rumors," he said. "Have you heard about Rachel Kraft yet?"

Her reaction said yes, but she said, "No."

Donald let it slide and explained the situation. He didn't detail the muder scene he had just come from, but he said that someone might have seen Rachel with the victim of a homicide.

"I need to know, Maddie," he said, resting his hand on the table near hers. "Do you have any idea where Rachel might be? Or maybe where she went?"

"No," she said, recoiling slightly. "Why would I know, Dad? She barely even talks to us."

"Us?" he asked.

She made a dismissive gesture. "Like, me or my friends. We don't really hang out with her."

"Do you remember the last time you saw her?"

Maddie stared at her fingers as she slowly pulled them away from her father's, making a fist. After a long pause, she said, "Friday night. At Cliff's party."

Before Donald could ask her to elaborate, she detailed the strange encounter she had with Rachel.

"She was acting super weird," Madison said.

"Weird how?"

She shrugged, acting annoyed. "I don't know…just, like, how she came up out of the ravine. And then starting talking about a bonfire." She shook her head. "We've never had a bonfire…"

Donald felt an itch in his throat, but he kept still and silent while Madison considered her next words. While he wasn't prone to jumping to conclusions or letting his imagination run wild, it felt too eerie that Rachel mentioned a bonfire.

Then again, she was a Kraft. Wouldn't she have heard the stories about Caroline? A young girl like Rachel—dressing in all black and keeping to herself—might think having a witch for an aunt was pretty damn cool. Maybe she had heard all the stories, and she decided to follow in Caroline's footsteps.

"Dad."

Donald realized he had been spacing out, staring at something beyond his daughter. He blinked and gave her a nod to show he was paying attention now.

"I'm sorry about this morning."

It had been a while since Donald had felt that sudden assault of pin-pricks behind the eyes that preceded an unexpected burst of emotion. He remembered seeing *My Girl* in the theater with Maddie a few years ago, and some of the scenes with Dan Aykroyd and his daughter summoned emotions similar to what he felt now.

"That's alright," he managed to say, coughing to cover up the breaking in his voice. "I told you, none of this has anything to do with you, Maddie. It's just...your mother and I—"

A knock at the door drew their attention as Eddie poked his head in.

"Sorry, partner, but I think we got something." He looked at Madison and gave a small wave. "Mind if I borrow him?"

"We'll talk tonight." Donald stood up and followed Eddie out into the administration office's lobby. He waited until Madison was on her way to class before he followed Eddie back into the conference room and closed the door.

"Who's Caroline Kraft?"

Donald snapped his head around to Eddie. The name never seemed to lose its power over him; it tightened his chest and made him feel like a rookie again.

Eddie motioned to the door. "I was in there, working the principal, and he made some comment about me not knowing the Krafts. I didn't want to give the impression that I was so far out of the loop here—which I am, by the way—so I acted like I was briefed on the 1974 suicide-slash-murder-slash-whatever the hell happened." He held up his hands in a "What gives?" gesture. "You couldn't have let me know there was a cold case involving one of our missing girl's relatives?"

Donald took a deep breath, ready for this day to be over. He held a hand up to keep Eddie's voice down. "There's nothing there, so don't push it. A girl died in 1974 and her surviving family left town—that's pretty much the only real facts that exist around that situation. So, you're not really out of the loop when it comes to Caroline Kraft."

"You don't think that's fucking relevant, man?!" Eddie was getting worked up, but at least he had the sense to do it in a whisper. "This girl and her mom come back to the town where a member of their family mysteriously died, and now we have another body?"

Looking at his watch, Donald saw that it was close to school letting out, meaning they'd get caught in heavy traffic if they stuck around. "Let's talk about it on the way back to the station," he said, hoping they wouldn't have to.

Aside from not wanting to revisit the darkest stain on a town he truly cared about, his mind was burdened by the divorce papers that awaited his signature at the end of this truly awful Monday.

After Barry Vickers watched the detectives leave through his office window, he slowly walked over to the tall file cabinet that stood against the wall opposite his framed pictures. He pulled open a middle drawer and moved all the racked files toward him, reaching behind them to draw out a wrinkled paper bag.

He carried the thing over to his desk and set it down ever so gently, as if it were old dynamite that might explode if handled poorly. After he lowered himself into his chair, he opened a desk drawer and took out a mostly empty bottle of whiskey, setting it next to the wrapped oddity.

"I'm sorry, Caroline," he said, with a voice heavy with aged remorse. "I should have told him...but..." He unscrewed the bottle, stared for a long moment at the paper bag that held something rectangular, and then drank the remaining contents of the bottle as if he were a man finding water in a desert.

He sat there staring at the item in his trembling hands, terrified to unwrap it. But when the last bell rang, he tore the old brown paper as if a gun had just gone off and he had a race to win.

The missing framed picture from 1974 had a grainy, twenty-year old image of the graduating class, which had been taken months before graduation (and Caroline Kraft's death).

Barry Vickers ran a finger along the rightmost edge of the frame, where twenty years ago his much-younger self flanked the sixty-five graduating students that made up Valley High's Class of 1974.

While Barry's vision had been failing more and more each year, a keen eye would be able to see his younger self rest his hand on Caroline Kraft's shoulder. The camera hadn't captured his other hand, which had been tenderly tracing the curve of the eighteen-year-old girl's spine.

"I'm legal now," she had said the first time she cornered him in this very office and slipped out of her long skirt. "You can have what you want."

"Don't," Barry mouthed in the present, echoing his past protests, useless as they had been.

Even all these years later, he felt entirely enthralled by the girl, unable to break free of whatever spell she had cast on him. He felt himself become aroused now, and he had to close his eyes and turn the picture over.

The darkness that would swallow Caroline two months after that photo had already taken root in the girl, and not for the first time Barry wondered if she had somehow passed it on to him through their carnal habits.

Allowing himself to open his eyes, Barry eyed the empty bottle, wondering if on the way home he should stop at the liquor store or the gun store.

Either would put him out of his misery, just one sooner than the other.

"You want to talk about it?"

Donald turned to Eddie in response, hoping the brief silence meant he might let the whole Caroline Kraft thing go. But his partner's eyes were on the envelope on Donald's lap—the divorce papers.

Donald, who had grabbed them when he got in the car because they had begun slipping farther between his seat and the console, now shoved them under his seat. "What's there to talk about?" Oddly enough, he decided he'd rather talk about 1974 than his failed marriage. "You believe in witches?"

Eddie laughed. "Is your wife really that bad?"

Despite his mood, Donald couldn't contain the snort of laughter. "I'm serious. You know, the Salem trials. Black magic. You believe in all that?"

"Eh," Eddie grunted, "part of me wants to. Believing in magic is easier than trying to figure out the real reasons why some of this awful shit happens in the world."

"Well," Donald said, turning back onto Parkview Avenue toward the station, "if you don't believe in witches, you won't find much to the Caroline Kraft case. Girl goes to a party held down in the ravine—kids used to love it down there. Bunch of high school seniors were all high or drunk and claimed they saw some huge monster strangle Caroline Kraft."

Eddie didn't have a snarky reply to that.

"Her body was found high up in a tree," Donald continued, "positioned all weird like some sort of ritual. None of the limbs were actually broken, but if you saw the crime scene photos—which Larson keeps buttoned up—you'd swear they were... People don't bend that way."

"Let me guess," Eddie said, looking out the passenger window as if not wanting Donald to see his face—as if it might betray how he processed these details. "There were a bunch of weird occurrences leading up to this? Animals born with two heads? Crops failing? Witchcraft was already in the local gossip?"

Donald honestly couldn't say. Whatever reports had survived that investigation were clearly audited to keep the case out of *The National Enquirer*. "I was too young at the time," he said, "but there was this old manor that the Kraft family owned—it's been sitting vacant since the murder..."

"So it was a murder then?" Eddie asked, turning back to face Donald.

"We used to call it haunted," Donald continued, ignoring the bait. "But it was just an old house. That's about the extent of what I knew about the Krafts back then. And when I joined the force, it was old news. My partner, Anne, worked it, but never wanted to talk about it—insisted it was a waste of time."

"We had a word for that in Charlotte," Eddie said, his voice sharp. "Coverup."

"This isn't Charlotte," Donald snapped back. "What do you think—you're going to come in here and shake this town up? Find something on a twenty-year-old cold case that my partner obsessed about for her entire career?"

Donald realized his voice was rising with his temper, but he had been pushed as far as he cared to be on a Monday—*Goddamn, I used to love Mondays,* he thought miserably.

"We'll find the girl," he added. "But she's not hiding in the past with her aunt. So leave it alone."

They ended their first day in silence.

CHAPTER 8
AFTER HOURS

E ddie really had nowhere else to go. His apartment still wasn't entirely furnished, and he didn't even have a TV yet. So, on his way home from the station, he found the nearest bar that served food.

He wasn't prone to dwelling on fate or luck (whether good or bad), but even he had to stop and consider if something more intentional than mere coincidence guided him to the place Tori Kraft worked.

The Narrow House earned its namesake through architectural necessity. Tucked between a much bigger drugstore and a run-down place bearing the sign *Jack Reed Attorney at Law*, the place had a cramped bar up front and a couple rows of tables near the back. The low lighting was welcoming, and Eddie appreciated the cozy decor—walls jam-packed with local memorabilia and scenic photos of the surrounding wilderness.

Tori caught sight of Eddie immediately and hurried over. "Detective Rane. Did you find her?"

Glancing around the bar, Eddie noticed that he was one of only three guests total. "Are you able to take a break? I wanted to talk a little."

That was clearly the wrong thing to say. Tori covered her mouth and her eyes widened as if expecting Eddie to tell her they found Rachel's body.

"No, it's nothing like that," Eddie reassured. "We're still on the case. We have units searching 'round the clock. I just wanted to talk to you about your daughter—see if there's anything we can use to help find her."

Tori lowered her hand and took a deep, ragged breath. "Jesus," she said. "Sorry... It's just... She hasn't been gone this long since we moved back."

Eddie put a comforting hand on her shoulder, feeling a boyish thrill that was almost alien to him after his two failed marriages and more one-night-stands than he cared to count. However, there was something electric about Tori Kraft, and when she reacted to his touch, Eddie suspected she might have felt the spark too.

"Let's sit for a few," he said softly. "I think the Monday night crowd here can survive without you, yeah?"

She breathed an awkward laugh and nodded. "Sure. Let me grab a couple beers."

"Maybe have the kitchen send something out," Eddie suggested. "Busy day—didn't have time to finish lunch."

"Sure," Tori said, giving him what she probably considered an easy smile—to Eddie it was dazzling. "Stacy makes the best burgers in Ransom. Grab a seat."

While Eddie waited for her at a high table in one of The Narrow House's dark corners, he observed two of the guests getting up to leave: a man and a woman casting suspicious glances at the new guy in town.

Despite the welcoming spirit he got from the bar itself, its patrons' looks immediately reminded Eddie that he was far from Charlotte. There was something about the people in this town that felt oppressive—as if they lived in fear of the outside world and would fight its influence tooth and nail.

Maybe that's why he felt so drawn to Tori. She was an outsider like him, and he supposed she was the only one he'd encountered in Ransom yet that didn't give off the impression that she was hiding something.

"Hope you don't mind a stout," Tori said, setting down two dark, chilled bottles bearing the label *The Crooked Creek Stout*. "We brew our own here, and I prefer my beer thick enough to eat with a spoon."

"A woman after my own heart." He reached for the bottle and took a sip—it was beautifully bitter and quite thick. In all honesty, he didn't drink a lot of stouts, but he was about as picky with beer as he was with burgers.

After taking her own sip, Tori set her bottle down and leaned toward Eddie. "So, I gave the woman at the station my statement—probably more detail than she expected. What else did you need to know?"

Eddie was a seasoned interrogator, and prided himself on being dexterous and adaptable when it came to getting information out of people. But something about the way Tori looked at him, he felt unable to form a logical series of questions.

"Regarding her past disappearances," Eddie began awkwardly, "seems like she's made a bit of a hobby out of running out on you. How would you describe your relationship with her?"

Tori sighed, staring into the contents of her bottle. "She's had a chip on her shoulder since her dad split. He was barely around when she was a kid, and I thought maybe she'd even be relieved that he took his moody ass down to Florida when she was seven. But part of me thinks she blames me for all of that."

"Were you married?"

She shook her head. "Just a stupid mistake. Tommy tried to play the martyr, making me feel guilty that he 'put his life on hold'—his words—so he could be a part-time dad. Like he was doing me this huge favor. We never even lived together though, and Rachel never even really talks about him anymore."

Eddie took another drink, considering the strange circumstances Rachel must have grown up in. He was empathetic toward Tori, but found that he was almost resentful toward Rachel, who was letting her rebellious behavior stress her mom out so much.

"But you guys get along alright?" Eddie pressed.

She gave a weak laugh. "I guess as good as a teenage girl and her mom can get along, sure. When we moved back here, things were good for a couple weeks, but then she leaned even further into just staying out and leaving me in the dark." Tori spun the bottle around so she could look at the label, which featured a graphic of the creek. "But she always comes back..."

A woman came by to drop off Eddie's burger and a basket of fries for Tori.

"Thanks, Stace. This is Detective Rane—new to Ransom. He's helping look for Rachel."

Stacy turned her kind, round face to Eddie and gave a smile. Her hair was tied back in a braid with a yellow bandana wrapped over her head. "I'm glad you're stepping in for the no-good sheriff."

Eddie couldn't help but smile at that and shook the woman's hand. "Good to meet you, Stacy. This looks delicious."

Once they were alone again, Eddie asked, "So, this is the longest she's been missing? A whole weekend?"

Tori kept her eyes on her beer, clearly not wanting to say. But after a moment, she did. "She was gone almost two weeks just before we moved here."

That seemed surprising to Eddie, considering how frantic Tori had been at the station this morning. If Rachel was truly prone to staying out, and had been gone for that long before, it seemed noteworthy that this recent vanishing had such an effect on Tori.

As if reading his thoughts, she turned her eyes to him. "You have to understand something about my daughter. I don't tell everyone this, because it might sound crazy—maybe I am crazy... But ever since Rachel was a toddler, she... How can I even explain this?" She took another drink before adding, "The kid's got a guardian angel or something, I don't know."

Eddie took another drink, hoping she would continue.

She did. "When she was seven and her dad moved away, I woke up and couldn't find her. We lived in an apartment, up on the second floor. I scrambled outside panicking, wondering if Tommy took her or something. But I just heard her voice while I was in the parking lot. '*Hi, Mommy.*'" Tori took another drink. "She was like fifty feet up—on the fucking roof of that place. Just looking down at me like it was totally normal."

Donald looked up at the roof of his old home. The gutters looked clogged with leaves from the huge maple tree that shaded the cozy, single-story house. He had an idiotic urge to go to his garage, grab his ladder, and actually solve a problem today.

But it wasn't his garage anymore, and today was certainly not a day for solving problems—the signed divorce papers under his arm were solid proof of that.

Without hesitation, he walked the path up to the front porch like a stranger and knocked on the door. In the brief silence that followed, he had the momentary hope that Laura was still at the office. But she appeared shortly after his knock and he felt a juvenile bitterness toward seeing her.

He used to find her so beautiful when she relaxed at home, but now, something about her disheveled hair and baggy top made her look sloppy to Donald. As petty as it was, he was at least relieved to not still be pining for something already lost.

Not wanting to drag it out, Donald held out the envelope. "You could have brought these over yourself. After our last talk, it was pretty clear it was coming."

Laura took the papers, hugging them to her chest. "It wasn't... Maddie volunteered, Don. I thought she just wanted to come talk to you."

He didn't tell her that she just left them on his porch. *Did she hope they might blow away?* Maybe that was her way to prevent the inevitable. *No,* he thought. Madison was too smart to think that would change anything. But it still bothered him, even if he logically knew that she was just a teenager and probably didn't know how better to deal with any of this.

Instead, he asked, "Is she here?"

Laura shook her head. "She went to Cassie's after school—Oh, before I forget. Anne stopped by looking for you a little bit ago. I gave her your new address."

He hadn't spoken to his old partner in a few days; she hadn't known about the upcoming divorce. He wasn't looking forward to having to catch the woman up on his recent life changes, but he did want to bend her ear a bit about the day's events.

Donald was going to turn to leave, but thought about what Maddie had said at school earlier. "Hey, Laura, have you ever seen that Kraft girl around here?"

Her face changed then. "Rachel Kraft?"

Donald explained the situation, each new detail deepening the furrows on his soon-to-be ex-wife's brow. He didn't mention Jonathan's murder, as that would likely trigger her notorious paranoia and his daughter would suffer the consequences.

When he was done describing Rachel's disappearance, Laura's gaze had become fixed on the sidewalk behind Donald. After a moment she said, "I didn't mention it before, because honestly I thought maybe I dreamt it or something..."

Donald waited for her to continue.

"About a week ago—maybe it was two weeks—Maddie was staying over Cassie's and there was a knock on the door around eight o'clock. It was Rachel Kraft. I only knew her because of that old estate of their family's... Tori was at the office signing some papers for it, and her daughter was very chatty.

"Anyway," Laura continued, blinking and looking at Donald now, "she asked if Maddie lived here. I said, 'Yeah, but she's at her friend's tonight,' and then shut the door." She repositioned herself and leaned closer to Donald. "The thing is, she just went and stood out there on the sidewalk, staring at the house. It was like she was just waiting for Maddie to get back. At around ten, I was going to bed, and she was still out there. I yelled out to her that Maddie wouldn't be home tonight, and she just said, 'Okay, thanks,' and kept standing there."

Donald turned as if Rachel were still there staring. "That is weird." He didn't know what else to say at the moment.

"Not as weird as when the doorbell rang at midnight," Laura said in barely a whisper. "That's the part that must have been a dream. Or maybe I had more wine than I thought. I went to answer the door, and no one was there. But I swore..." She laughed, shaking her head. "I swear I saw someone standing on the roof of the neighbor's house..."

Eddie offered to walk Tori home, noticing how much their conversation had shaken her. She put up a half-hearted refusal, saying she made the walk every night, but Eddie could tell she would prefer the company. She smiled when he said he really didn't mind getting a look at the rest of the town.

They each had two more stouts before her shift actually ended, and by the time they reached the Krafts' trailer, Eddie's better judgement had already taken its leave and he had accepted her invitation to come in.

When she kissed him inside on her small couch, it took everything Eddie had to pull away from her and say, "You alright just sitting here awhile?"

Her smile was even brighter then.

With his arm around her, he cradled her head to his shoulder.

She fell asleep within seconds.

Despite Laura mentioning giving Anne Warren his address, Donald was still surprised to see his partner waiting for him on the stoop of his apartment.

"If I had known you'd be here staking out my place, I wouldn't have stopped for a drink," Donald said, carrying his jacket over his shoulder.

Anne looked tired, leaning against the door to his place with a folder tucked under one arm. She pushed herself toward him and gave him a comforting hug.

"Sorry to hear about Laura," she whispered. Donald could smell that she had stopped for a drink as well.

"I'm sure you're less shocked than I was about it," he said with a small laugh. "We both know I only got married because of Madison. It's a miracle we lasted this long."

"Still," Anne said, patting him solidly on the back, "hate that you have to go through it. Hope Maddie's dealing alright."

Donald bit back his reply—he knew his daughter wasn't taking it well, but he also knew that kids were much more resilient than adults with stuff like this. So he just nodded and said, "I think so." He pulled back so he could read Anne's face. "Shouldn't you be on a cruise or something? Retirement's just getting started and you're hanging around my place on a Monday night?"

Anne gave one of her rare, crooked smiles. Standing eye to eye with Donald, Anne was a tall woman with broad shoulders, who once had to almost look down at her partner. Now, she had a sunken posture, as if carrying all the baggage from her thirty years on the force had finally begun weighing her down.

"I missed you, partner." She nodded toward the door. "I've been standing out here for about an hour—how about you invite me in, stud?"

Donald led her inside. "Can I get you something to drink?"

"I'll have whatever you're having," she said. "Mind if I smoke?"

This, combined with the alcohol on Anne's breath, made Donald pause while reaching for the bourbon. Anne had been quitting smoking during Donald's first year on the force, and he remembered vividly how difficult it was for her. But when she kicked it, she kicked it for good.

Or so he had thought.

"Sure," he said, grabbing a couple rocks glasses from the cabinet above his makeshift bar—which was really just a space next to his apartment's stove where he kept one bottle of bourbon and an unopened bottle of red wine.

Anne sparked her lighter and puffed on a Camel, filling the corner of Donald's dim, pathetic apartment with smoke. "I heard about Keene," she said between drags.

Donald set the two glasses and the bottle of bourbon on the coffee table and took a seat on the couch next to Anne. His eyes were fixed on the folder next to their drinks. "I'm surprised, considering Larson snatched it from us—even though we were already investigating his disappearance."

Anne took another long drag of her cigarette, the glow from its tip deepening the aged creases of her face. Her gaze was distant, staring into the past.

"You know, I still remember the Kennedy assasination." Her voice was as listless as her gaze now. "I was in high school...I think senior year. Hit me hard, just like everyone else. But it wasn't just the killing, ya know?" She took another drag. "It was what followed. I don't think Kennedy was cold in the ground before people started coming up with all these wild theories: second gunman, deep state, that fucking grassy knoll." She gave a detached sigh. "No one could live with the horrible truth of what happened, so they thought creating shadows behind the trigger might make it easier."

Not sure what to say, Donald poured out two drinks while Anne continued to smoke.

"I think that's why I never let myself look into Keene."

Donald froze at that, his gaze pulled to the folder again, somehow knowing what it contained now.

Anne produced an ashtray from her pocket and set it on the table next to her drink. "I didn't want to be like all those people." She picked up her glass and downed all of its contents. "I didn't want Caroline Kraft's ghost hanging over me while we chased shadows that weren't there."

"Did you think Keene was involved in Caroline's death?" Donald asked, sipping his own drink while pouring Anne another one.

"Her murder?" Her eyes found him now, sharp and narrowed. "He was there at least, I know that." She counted off names with the fingers on one hand. "Vandrel. Dupree. Windsor. Collins, or Harris back then. All of them. The Remains, they called themselves." Anne laughed at that, but didn't smile. She threw back the next bourbon and poured her own this time.

Donald didn't press her; he knew how she got. She would tell him what all this meant at her own pace. He just hoped she was coherent by then, because even he had trouble keeping it together after that much liquor.

She ashed her cigarette again and tapped a finger on the folder. "He wrote the article about Caroline's death. Even back then, with everything going on, I remember thinking... Why the hell would the *Ransom Courier* have a goddamn high school senior—who was only working at the paper on a work-study program—write about the death of Walter fucking Kraft's granddaughter?" She laughed again, in a way that actually frightened Donald. "That should have been national news, not a school project for some dipshit who I'm almost positive was at that fuckin' party."

Donald had never heard Anne swear so much. When he first met her, she had the presence of a methodical minister. But now she was every bit the grizzled private eye who had seen one too many unsolved cases—the type of character Donald aspired to be as a child, when he'd watch old noir movies with his dad.

But he had absolutely no desire to be like the character he sat next to now.

"And the Krafts are back now." Anne smashed her cigarette in the ashtray and polished off her next bourbon. "And I don't think it's chasing shadows anymore to ask the hard questions when Jonathan Keene shows up dead while Caroline's niece is nowhere to be found."

Standing up, Anne pointed to the folder again. "That's just the appetizer, Donnie boy. Once you and that new partner of yours look into it, maybe we should talk again. Just ask yourself: How did Keene know what wasn't in the police reports?"

Unable to restrain his curiosity any longer, Donald flipped the folder open as Anne left his apartment. Atop several reports and notebook pages, there was an old newspaper clipping.

Ransom Courier – March 17, 1974 *By Jonathan Keene, Staff Contributor*

Local Teen Found Dead in Sycamore Hollow

RANSOM CREEK, NC — The quiet of Ransom Creek was shaken this weekend after the body of *Caroline Kraft*, 18, a student at Valley High School, was discovered early Saturday morning in the wooded area beyond Sycamore Hollow.

Kraft, a senior known for her relation to the late Walter Kraft, was last seen late Friday night near Ridgeback Trail. According to the sheriff's department, a small gathering of students had taken place in the woods earlier that evening, but most attendees claimed they didn't realize Caroline had wandered off until much later.

Her body was discovered shortly after dawn, elevated nearly twenty feet in a tree. Authorities have not made an official determination, but initial reports describe bruising on the neck and limbs contorted in a manner that may be consistent with a fall.

Sheriff Walter Rourke stated, "At this point, we're investigating this as a tragic accident. There is no current evidence to suggest criminal activity, though the unusual positioning of the body does raise questions."

Vice Principal Barry Vickers, speaking on behalf of Valley High, said, "Caroline was quiet. She mostly kept to herself. We've reached out to her family and fellow students to offer support. She will be dearly missed."

Students who were present at the gathering declined to speak on the record, but one classmate, requesting anonymity, said the group had dared Caroline to explore the burn pile near the Hollow—a longtime source of local ghost stories and teen lore. "She said she heard something moving in the trees," the student recalled. "No one took her seriously."

Though details remain unclear, the event has reignited concern over unsupervised teenage activity in the parkland area near the creek.

Caroline's family has requested privacy during this time. A small service will be held later this week.

Editor's note: *Sycamore Hollow has been the site of multiple incidents involving local youth in the last decade. The Courier advises all residents to avoid the area after dark.*

CHAPTER 9
HEIR TO THE ASHES

Deborah Collins hadn't expected to cry. When she heard Jonathan Keene was back in town over the weekend, she wanted nothing more than to burst into the lodge, pound on his door, and slap the shit out of him for what he'd done back in '76.

Now, she wished she could have instead gone to him on her knees, doing anything it took to convince the man to whisk her away to a big city, away from her life in Ransom Creek forever.

"Mom?"

Debbie snapped out of her trance, grabbing a tissue from the box on her luxurious vanity and wiping away snot and tears. "What, hon?"

There was a soft tap on the door before it clicked open. Her daughter's blonde hair spilled through as she peeked in. "Cliff's coming to get me for school. I probably won't be home until late—we're going to the mall after school to hang out with friends."

Keeping her back toward the door, Debbie waved a hand to Valerie. "Okay, I'll probably be at the Kraft place until late, so make sure you let Dad know where you're going."

"I told him when he left," she called from down the hall, already on her way downstairs.

Debbie closed her eyes and took a deep breath, struggling to find some sense of calm while trying not to picture Trevor plowing his secretary. Her husband was a terrible sneak, leaving multiple glaring trails of evidence that led to his various infidelities. His most recent hobby was going into the office extremely early to work on the budget when Debbie knew perfectly well he was bending Jenny over her desk before the rest of the bankers arrived to work.

In all honesty, Trevor's pathetic sexual deviances hardly bothered her anymore. What did bother her was the charade they had to keep up as one of the premier power couples in Ransom Creek: her, a thriving real estate mogul, and him, president of First National Bank of Ransom. Together, the Collinses were an installation in town, and they made plenty of sacrifices to keep up appearances.

Debbie pulled another tissue from the box and finished wiping away the unexpected sorrow she felt for Jonathan Keene. Looking in the mirror, she saw a ruined woman doing her best to hold it together; something about that made her smile, and she carried that feeling through the rest of her morning routine.

She left the house and drove her Mercedes-Benz down the gently winding road of Potter's Glen. Of all the nicer neighborhoods in Ransom Creek, theirs was by far the most expensive and most prestigious. However, Debbie had grown to despise the exact nature of the place; everything was too simple and clean.

Something deep down inside of her craved ruin, and she suspected that's what the news of Jonathan's murder had awakened. She proceeded out of her neighborhood, across Parkview Avenue, and through downtown.

She arrived at the Kraft estate to find Marcus' Lexus parked along the carriage loop that led up to the manor's front door. Normally, she might have thought it odd that her top investor would be at one of her properties first thing in the morning. But in light of recent events, she half-expected to find him here.

After parking her car, she hurried up the porch's seven steps and pushed open the great door leading to the huge, vacant, dead home.

"Marcus?" Her voice echoed like a wandering ghost through the place, and despite the morning sunlight, she felt properly spooked. Normally, her visits to this old place were made in silence; she even took her cell phone calls outside because she didn't like the sound of her voice bouncing off those cursed walls.

Nobody answered her echoing voice now, so she closed the door and proceeded toward the basement stairs. She thought the place felt cold, but certainly it was just her imagination. It was already seventy degrees outside and it was barely past 9 a.m.

"Are you alone?"

The voice startled her just as she placed one of her high heels on the first step downstairs. "Yes. Marcus, what are you doing here?" She knew the answer to that question, but was curious to hear his excuse. It was unlikely he would use her own reason for the visit: to see if Jonathan Keene had been here looking for something.

Marcus didn't answer, so she descended the carpeted stairs to join him. The basement lights were off, but the high windows let enough light in to illuminate the storage space. All of the Kraft estate's inventory was kept down here, neatly organized in sealed boxes and trunks. Debbie stepped into the main room to see Marcus knelt over such a box, pulling accordion files out and stacking them haphazardly on the floor.

"He was here," Marcus said, not looking at her. "Did you let him in?"

She looked up the stairs as if someone were behind her, but when she realized the question was for her she spat back, "Why the hell would I let that bastard in here?" Debbie tried to make the words sound believable, but even her own ears could tell how hollow they sounded. Her throat was still tight with restrained sorrow over Jon's death.

Marcus turned to face her, still keeping his knee on the ground to continue his digging. "I know he called you, Debbie. I have his phone. So just tell me: Did you let him in?"

Debbie didn't have to force the hard expression she gave him. "Of course not. He called me to catch up, but I wouldn't let him sift through all this. I know our arrangement, and I wouldn't jeopardize the deal. I need this inheritance to go through just as much as you do."

Holding her gaze for a moment, Marcus seemed to accept that. He let out a sort of hiss between his clenched teeth before continuing his search.

"What the hell are you looking for?"

Without turning, Marcus dug in his back pocket and produced a folded note. He held it out for Debbie, who took it hesitantly.

Unfolding the page, she saw it was a typed page from a book. She knew it was written by Jon even before she saw the block letters at the top: *WHAT REMAINS - JONATHAN KEENE*. A header indicated this was the beginning of chapter four, and Debbie—almost in a trance—read it aloud.

Chapter 4 - His Heir Apparent

Walter Kraft's ashes were what originally poisoned the creek.

Even if you don't believe in the supernatural, you wouldn't have been able to walk through Sycamore Hollow when the moon was high and rationally explain the dark oppression that would settle over you.

In retrospect, it's no wonder the Vandrels were drawn to this place. Marcus said his ancestors had been all over the world searching for signs of Adratheon. He would often ask me when we were in the ravine, "You can feel him, right?"

I did, but I played the skeptic. Marcus Vandrel had a way of owning you once you gave him your conviction. He may have owned the other members of the Remains by then, but I withheld.

That is, until we found the burn pit.

It didn't seem logical—the legend around Walter Kraft's pyre was such an institution in Ransom Creek, you would have figured the site of it would have either been found by that point or at least falsely established. But there was no doubt in my mind when Debbie and I came across that site...

Walter Kraft burned his fortune there and tried to force his eldest son to watch. I know how crazy it sounds—maybe not as crazy as other things in this book—but I swear, when I touched those ashes, I saw everything.

Ransom Creek. 1968. Walter Kraft is a hale middle-aged man in a fine tailored suit. He looks out of place in the ravine, but the commanding aura he exudes makes it seem like his surroundings are more in the wrong than he.

Walter tosses another log on the pyre, whistling some jaunty tune. Behind him, tied to the tree with a gag in his mouth, his eldest son, Jeremiah, thrashes against the tight ropes that hold him. A shadow creeps up behind the two, unseen and unheard.

The entire Kraft fortune was piled under the kindling, awaiting the flames.

I saw it all.

When I blinked that vision away, I saw the ashes in my hand, and I knew they were meant for me. We hid them in a box—

"Where the hell is it?!"

Debbie was jolted back to the present. She hadn't intended to read the entire page, but Jonathan's writing had transported her back to her senior year of high school, when she was Deborah Harris and they had found that burn pit. The same emotions had dug their roots into her and she shivered.

"Where's what?"

Marcus spun on her, fury in his eyes. "The box! That's what he's talking about. Those ashes you both took from the pit. The ceremony needed all of the remains. But you two put some in a box."

Debbie didn't follow. "Why would it be here? I never saw it after that night. Jonathan insisted on keeping it."

"Everything comes back here!" Marcus motioned to the neatly organized boxes and totes, all containing the remaining bits and pieces of the Kraft estate that Walter's surviving descendants were set to inherit in ten months. "You think he'd take them anywhere else?"

His eyes widened as he stepped toward Debbie. "I know he called you. There's no way he'd come back here and not reach out. Did you bring him here?"

The accusation startled her. In truth, Debbie was indeed drawn here, hoping to see some sign that Jon had been by. But she certainly hadn't met with him. "No, I told you! He just wanted to catch up—he sounded...I don't know, nostalgic." She stepped past Marcus, not liking the way he looked at her. She pulled a box flap back to inspect the contents. "And I haven't been down here since we moved all this in."

Marcus' cellular phone rang. He made a grunt as he pulled it from his pocket; a soft beep told Debbie he had declined the call. "It has to be here." He was calmer now, but his anger had not yet subsided.

Now that her heart rate had slowed to a normal rhythm, questions began formulating in her mind. "If you know it's here, what's the problem? Jon's dead."

Saying the words nearly made her sob again, but adrenaline kept the tears at bay. There was a confrontation to be had; she was never one to back down from an argument, which had been precisely why she and Jonathan Keene never worked out.

Marcus turned back to her and pointed toward the page still in her hand. "You think that's the only page, Deb? He was writing a goddamn book about us—"

"I can see that, Marcus," she snapped. "Jesus Christ, he warned you he would, didn't he? Is that why he came here?" The question suddenly put the pieces together in her mind. "Was he threatening you with releasing this?" She held up the page from Jonathan's book. "Was he blackmailing you?"

Marcus just glared at her as his phone rang again. Instead of answering her, he pulled the phone out, pressed a button, and snarled into it. "What?!"

While Marcus listened to whatever the caller said, Debbie looked at the page again. The scene Jonathan had written was a memory she had never forgotten—it occasionally came to her in dreams, waking her up in a cold sweat. She wasn't lying though: she never knew what he did with that box of ashes.

"No, Roger!" Marcus snapped. "I do not want you to go to the fucking police! Larson's dealing with the murder—No, Roger! Just stay out of it! I'll come by later. Just don't talk to anyone about it. And stop calling me."

After he hung up, Marcus stepped toward Debbie. "Find the box, Debbie. Until we find out who killed Jonathan, it's a loose end for both of us. Do you understand?" He narrowed his eyes, and for a moment Deborah thought he might strike her, or worse. But he just added, "Without those ashes, we may as well burn this place down."

Despite the strong desire to push back, she nodded, because she did, in fact, understand that the ashes tied her (and each member of the Remains) to Jonathan's death, as well as Caroline Kraft's. As much as she wanted to argue with Marcus, now was not the time.

"I'll find them," she said. "Just tell me..."

He kept his slitted eyes on her, waiting.

"Did you kill him?"

Marcus didn't flinch. In fact, the corner of his mouth twitched in what might have been a smile.

"Funny," he said. "I was going to ask you the same thing."

She waited until he left before she cried again.

CHAPTER 10
AN UNPLANNED VISIT

Eddie tried to get to the station early, but he was on foot and had to swing by his apartment for a change of clothes. By the time he made it in, Donald's car was already in the lot. He hurried to his desk, bypassing some chit-chat with Beth, who had been staring at the empty lobby like a kid waiting for the school bell to ring.

He found Donald at the desk next to his own, scribbling furiously in his notebook as he pinned a phone between his head and shoulder.

"—okay, and that was two weeks ago?" Donald looked up when he saw Eddie begin to sit down. "Sure," he said, nodding for Eddie to come around to him. "No, that's great. I appreciate all the information. I'll forward it all to the sheriff's office right away."

Eddie looked around the bullpen, noticing that no one else was around to hear his partner's big fat lie. He took a seat on the edge of Donald's desk and said, "Sorry I'm late," at the same time as Donald said, "You're late."

However, Donald didn't seem to notice—or more likely he did notice and didn't want to acknowledge it for whatever reason. Instead, he hung up the phone and began tucking his notebook back into his jacket.

"Let's go."

Eddie motioned toward the phone. "Who was that?"

Donald looked over his shoulder toward the chief's office. The door was shut and the lights were off. "I'll tell you in the car. We're going to the mayor's office."

Once they were safely outside, Eddie asked, "So, what's at the mayor's office? Figured we'd be going back to the high school and round up your daughter's friends from that party."

"We will," Donald said, slipping on his sunglasses. "But that was Jonathan Keene's boss at *The Globe*—a guy named Jackie Schmidt. Sounded like a leprechaun." He paused while they got into the car, turning to Eddie as he added, "Apparently, Keene was acting pretty erratic for the past few weeks. Took a forced vacation."

"Interesting," Eddie said, drumming his fingers on the passenger door. "Any mention of what triggered it?"

Donald shook his head, turning on the ignition. "Didn't sound like he and Jackie were close friends. But he did mention something about Jonathan missing recent deadlines—working on some new book. Caused some conflict between them."

Eddie remembered something then, his fingers leaving a rhythm unfinished. "The satchel."

"What's that?"

"At the crime scene," Eddie said, his eyes focused on the car's dash as Donald backed out of the lot. "There was that leather satchel—I told you old authors used to use them. My uncle wrote books, and he always put his manuscripts in them. Some kind of superstitious thing with authors... I always just figured he was pretentious."

Donald motioned to get on with it. "What about it? We already figured there was a book missing."

Eddie looked at him. "I'm just saying, a journalist comes back to his hometown while working on a book that was worth risking his job over, yeah? Couldn't we assume the book was about this place—or more likely, someone in this place."

"Killed over a book?" Donald mused aloud, turning down Parkview. "Must have been a pretty bad book."

The laugh they shared was darker than the sky as a morning storm rolled in.

The drive to the mayor's office was brief, but by the time the detectives parked it was already pouring. Donald turned off the engine but left the AC on so they could wait out the worst of it.

"So," Eddie said, his fingers drumming again. "What's this have to do with our actual case? Is Rachel something to the mayor?" The memory of Tori's breath on his neck made him shift in his seat. "Her mom?"

Donald was staring at the courthouse steps, his head low as if the rain were oppressive even through the windshield. "Well, that party that Rachel crashed on Friday was at the Windsor place. Benjamin Windsor is the city planner..."

It made sense to Eddie that they would follow up on the last place Rachel was seen, but something about that phone call that Donald had intercepted bothered him. "Am I missing some connection here, Don?"

"Don't call me Don."

But Eddie kept going. "You take a call meant for the sheriff's office—"

"I didn't take it," Donald interrupted. "Schmidt didn't know the police department was different from the sheriff's office. That's on him."

"—and almost immediately afterward you want to hit up the city planner instead of starting with his kid, who your daughter put there at the scene, right?" Eddie, who was pointing the details out on the dashboard, turned to Donald with upturned hands, eager for explanation. "Lay it out for me."

Donald removed his sunglasses and looked into Eddie's eyes. "How much do you know about Bright Hollow?"

The question and the way it was asked made Eddie recoil, as if somehow Donald knew about him staying with Tori last night. "The trailer park?"

Donald nodded, raising his eyebrows. "Marcus Vandrel. His realty development company proposed that project just last year. It went before the town council, where plenty of attendees objected to affordable housing on this side of the creek." He snapped his fingers. "But Benjamin Windsor approves it almost immediately."

Eddie felt his eyebrows furrow as if on their own accord. "Sounds like Vandrel knows how to grease palms. Again, what's that got to do with our subject?"

Donald held his gaze. "Guess who was the first resident of Bright Hollow."

Lightning struck outside, followed immediately by a peal of thunder. And yet, the rain was already starting to die down.

Eddie watched as Donald turned back toward the courthouse and reached for the keys still in the ignition. His movements were slow, as if he were trying to stall himself.

"There's something else, isn't there?" Eddie asked. "I mean, I'm just as curious as you to find out if this Windsor guy knows something about why Keene was here and what it might have to do with our missing girl. But I can tell there's something else."

Reaching for the door handle, Donald paused for a beat. "Tori Kraft was a kid when she left Ransom—I was about the same age. That was when her aunt was found dead under very suspicious circumstances in the ravine. But Jonathan Keene was eighteen years old, working for *The Ransom Courier* as a student reporter."

"Let me guess," Eddie interjected. "Benjamin's daddy ran the paper?"

"Charles Windsor ran everything," Donald replied, nodding toward the courthouse. "He even had a short stint as mayor before he died from lung cancer—dude smoked like a goddamn chimney. But yeah, old Chuck started out in print media, acting as editor-in-chief of *The Ransom Courier* from the years 1968 to about 1976, when he switched lanes to local politics."

Eddie followed Donald out of the car then. The sudden storm was all but gone. "I'm guessing little Benny was in that ravine then? And daddy didn't really want that to be public knowledge."

Donald nodded, leading them toward the courthouse steps. "That's my thinking. Regardless, there may be a connection to the Krafts, which might explain why Rachel was at their place Friday night."

Seemed like a solid thread to Eddie, but the rational, investigative part of his mind was at odds with the strange vision that Tori had put in his head last night—the one in which a young Rachel Kraft seemingly magicked herself up to a third-story roof in order to stare at her mother like a zombie.

For a brief moment, as he ascended the stairs one step behind his new partner, Eddie considered sharing that little gem. But he didn't feel particularly eager to even mention that he had spoken to Tori Kraft last night—it would open too many doors.

Instead, he just walked through the one Donald held open for him.

Benjamin Windsor was finally just getting comfortable at his desk when his secretary buzzed him.

"The police?"

"Yes, sir," Suzanne replied in a hushed voice, as if worried she might be arrested if she spoke too loudly. "Would you like me to send the detectives in?"

Detectives? he thought, knowing that Larson would have sent over his own deputies if this was regarding Keene's murder. "Tell them to have a seat while I finish up a call," Benjamin replied.

He heard Suzanne begin to say that he'd be right with them before the line died. Benjamin grabbed the phone and punched in Patrick's number. After several rings, he grunted in frustration and hung up. If the sheriff was out on a call, he wasn't about to go through dispatch to reach him.

Benjamin called Debbie next, but got her voicemail. He slammed the phone down harder, frustration growing. Fortunately, one of the Remains answered.

"Why are the cops here, Roger?" Benjamin could hear his oldest friend breathing, but not answering. "Roger?!"

"Listen, Ben. Something's going on with Marcus..."

Benjamin looked at his office door as if the detectives were about to kick it down. "Fuck Marcus! Just tell me what the cops are doing here, Roger? Pat's handling the murder, right?"

"That's what I'm trying to tell you," Roger said. His voice was low and constrained. "The Kraft girl's missing. One of my housekeepers told the goddamn detectives looking for her that she saw Rachel with Jon. They're probably there to ask you about her."

Squeezing the phone so tightly that he could hear the plastic creak under his grip, Benjamin barely restrained himself from smashing it against the desk. *The fucking girl!* He hadn't even thought about how that wrinkle might come back on him. *Cliff just had to have a goddamn party!*

"Ben." Roger's voice sounded even lower now. "Whatever they ask about, do not mention the Rothen deal. We don't—"

"To hell with Rothen!" Benjamin lunged to his feet as if ready for a fight. He struggled to contain his anger, not wanting to shout with the cops outside his door "You think Rothen's going to pull the trigger if there's another goddamn scandal involving that goddamn family—after we finally rid this town of them?! You get your ass over here, Roger. Immediately."

He hung up and took several deep breaths before going to his door.

"Detectives," Benjamin said with a fake smile. Not for the first time, he felt like he should win an Academy Award for his ability to placate city officials. "Come on in and let me know what I can do for you."

He recognized Donald Avery as the pair stood up, but the other one looked like some sort of hipster that drove a school bus for a living; his hair was too long in the back and his scruffy face bore a thick mustache and a pair of cocky eyes.

Benjamin led them into his office after telling Suzanne to hold his calls.

"Sorry for the wait," he said, taking a seat behind his desk while Donald produced a notebook and pen from his jacket. "It's been pretty hectic here since what happened yesterday—but I'm sure I don't have to tell you guys."

"You have our condolences," the new guy said, drumming his fingers on his chair's armrest.

Benjamin tensed. He thought he heard sarcasm in that smarmy bastard's voice. But he could tell from the man's reaction that it was probably just paranoia; he seemed sincere.

"I heard you were friends with the victim," the slob continued.

Giving him the most condescending smile he could muster, Benjamin said, "I'm sorry, and you are?"

He smiled. "Detective Eddie Rane. Just transferred from Charlotte."

"Well, Detective Rane, I'm not sure where you heard that, but I haven't even spoken to Jonathan Keene in probably twelve years. When he left Ransom, we weren't on the best of terms." He turned to Donald. "I'm sure you haven't stayed friends with all the guys you chummed around with in high school."

Donald seemed uninterested in the discussion, maybe even bothered by his partner's comments. "Well, we were actually hoping to speak to you about Rachel Kraft. We heard she was at your home briefly on Friday night."

Benjamin was prepared and certainly didn't flinch this time. "Yeah, I understand she's disappeared again. Her poor mom. But you'd have to ask my son about that—I can't keep up with his friends. We were out pretty late on Friday." He glanced at Rane when he added, "At a function with Mayor O'Brien."

"That's alright," Donald replied with a nod, "we'll make sure to speak with your son about the party. While we're here, would you mind telling us what you know about Victoria Kraft?"

"The mother? I know she hasn't been here much longer than your partner here, but it seems like her kid isn't having the easiest time settling in." Benjamin leaned back in his chair and raised his hands in a shrug. "Unfortunately, I haven't had the pleasure of meeting her, so my knowledge ends there."

Donald motioned with his hand as if there were more to tell. "But you were aware she originally moved away when her aunt died, only to return once your Bright Hollow development opened up."

Benjamin straightened in his chair but kept his face passive. "Well, it's not *my* development, Detective. I just approved it. That's the Vandrel Group's project, so you can ask Marcus about any rental agreements with the Kraft woman."

"So, we're correct in assuming you didn't have a stake in Bright Hollow, correct?" Detective Rane asked, slouching in his chair like the disrespectful bum that Benjamin had immediately taken him for. "Figured since you greenlit the development despite the council's objections, Vandrel must have made one hell of a pitch."

It took everything Benjamin had to remain calm and force a careless grin. "Obviously, no, I didn't have a stake—that'd be a massive abuse of office. Whatever the council thinks of him, Marcus Vandrel's made great strides in diversifying Ransom Creek. Bright Hollow was a necessary step in offering affordable housing without affecting any surrounding property values." He shrugged with his hands again. "How could we not approve it?"

Donald jotted something down in his notebook before asking, "Do you stay in regular contact with Marcus Vandrel?"

Benjamin nodded. "It's hard to avoid big real estate developers in my line of work. He also the mayor's biggest donor."

Detective Rane propped one of his dirty green sneakers up on his knee as he said, "He was another high school chum, right?"

"You could say that," Benjamin offered, not liking where this was going.

Rane picked at a nail—a clear mock display of detachment. "Did he also have a falling out with Jonathan Keene?"

Benjamin let the question hang there a moment before turning back to Donald. "What's this about, Avery? I thought Sheriff Larson was investigating the Keene murder. What's any of this have to do with your case?"

Donald gave his partner a sidelong look before turning back to Benjamin. He leaned forward in his chair. "Sorry, Mr. Windsor. We just have reason to believe that the Kraft girl's disappearance may be linked to Jonathan Keene's murder. While we're not investigating the murder, we were investigating Keene's disappearance up until his body turned up."

"And your buddy was at the scene," Rane added. This time he was clearly being antagonistic, but Benjamin wouldn't take the bait.

"I suppose you'll have to take that up with him," Benjamin suggested. "Marcus has interests all over town, so I'm not surprised that he'd be first in line to speak with Sheriff Larson after a dead body turns up near one of his parks."

He let that hang for a moment as Donald Avery jotted down more notes. Eddie Rane just stared at Benjamin, smirking and waiting.

Finally, Benjamin stood up. "Well, if there isn't anything else..."

Donald closed his notebook and reached out to shake Benjamin's hand. "Appreciate your time. Have a good rest of your day."

Benjamin Windsor did not have a good rest of his day.

CHAPTER 11
DIVIDED

"Well, he's clearly full of shit."

Donald bit back his reply, waiting for Eddie to close his door so he could pull out of the courthouse lot. Once they were back on Parkview, Donald said, "You can't do that here."

"Do what? Our job?"

Donald rolled down his window, hoping he could cool off. The brief storm left a mugginess that was amplified by Donald's mood. "It's not our job to treat city officials as mobsters. We have nothing on Benjamin Windsor, aside from the fact that his son had a party."

"Don't tell me you believe he's not tighter with that Vandrel guy than he's letting on." Eddie's voice had an edge to it. "I don't care how much money you have—you don't fast track something like a trailer park in a town like this, especially when the council's not on board. Not unless someone goes to bat for you."

All the little annoyances from yesterday were coming back to Donald now, and he gripped the steering wheel tighter. "Doesn't matter what I believe. Rattling a guy that close to the goddamn mayor won't get us any closer to finding the girl. Unless you have reason to believe he kidnapped her?"

Eddie turned in his seat. "Hold up, man. You were the one linking Keene to Windsor—you brought this to light, so don't act like I'm going in all half-cocked."

"I shared a hunch, Rane. You know we don't act on hunches until we have some substance." He turned the car into the city hall parking lot.

"What the hell are we doing here?" Eddie asked.

Donald was quicker to turn off the car and get out this time. Before slamming the door shut, he said, "Getting some fucking substance."

Madison Avery drew the page out of her pocket again. The edges were starting to fray from how much she had been handling it since last night. She couldn't stop reading the scene, feeling that same sense of foreboding that gripped her the first time she had read it.

It was almost as if the words themselves weren't what bothered her. Instead, it was the eerie sense that Rachel had somehow intended for her to read it; for what reason, she couldn't begin to guess.

Madison smoothed the paper out on her lap. Sitting in the stall in the dimly lit back corner of the girls' restroom, she was as alone as she was likely to get in Valley High during the middle of a school day. But she still hunched over the cryptic document so whatever ghosts haunting that particular toilet couldn't read over her shoulder.

When her gaze focused, Madison's heart stopped. Had she somehow grabbed a different piece of paper? She flipped it over: blank. Turning it back, she scanned the words that were all foreign—not in the sense that they were from a different language, but because she had read the scene so many times since yesterday that she knew what they said almost verbatim.

But these words were different.

The story was different.

Instead of narrating a scene about teenagers at a party, a missing bonfire, and a dark presence lurking across the creek, Madison read a scene about a girl sitting alone in a restroom stall. The girl was scared, worried that the dark presence from the creek had followed her through the school halls, cornering her in the restroom.

Madison's pulse quickened with each word, disbelieving how descriptive the prose was in describing Rachel Kraft's shoes as they dragged along the restroom floor toward the stall. The narrator's terror was her own, and Madison had to forcefully keep her eyes on the page so they wouldn't flick up to peer between the stall's cracks, looking for Rachel's silhouette.

In the scene, Rachel just stood there, breathing heavily, uncoiling a noose that tumbled softly to the floor. This time, Madison did look up, but there was nothing outside her door. But when she resumed reading, she actually heard the breathing and her racing heart stopped as she sucked in a breath.

The last line of the page was: *Rachel gripped the noose tightly, ready to choke the Remains from Ransom Creek for good, before slamming her fist against the stall door.*

A loud bang shook the stall door, eliciting a shriek from Madison as she slid off the side of the toilet to be as far from Rachel Kraft as she could.

But the stall door was still closed and there were no feet standing on the other side. Madison was still alone.

Feeling ridiculous and disgusting, Madison struggled out of the tight confines, trying not to touch the toilet. However, her eyes caught the page and she gasped. Without thinking, she wadded it up, tossed it in the still water, and flushed.

Not staying to wash her hands, she shouldered her backpack on and hurried to the hall. As she made her way to English class, she tried to assure herself she had imagined everything. There was no way the page could have changed from the party Friday night, to Rachel in the restroom, and then back to the party.

It just wasn't possible.

However, it was no good. She could not convince herself that she had hallucinated it all. It was just too real. And now she couldn't even prove it one way or the other, since she had flushed the damn thing.

By the end of English class—which she completely spaced—Madison Avery had come to terms with the fact that something terrible had happened to Rachel Kraft, and she might be the only one who knew.

Eddie groaned as he pushed another cardboard box back onto the wired shelf. "If I have to review one more goddamn conditional use permit for a porch extension, man, I'm going to burn this place down."

Donald ignored the complaint, flipping diligently through files in his own similar box. Eddie found himself even more agitated since it looked like his partner was actually enjoying this process.

Leaning back to stretch his cramped spine, Eddie asked, "Why don't we just ask someone here if they know where the forms are?"

No answer; Donald just continued to flip through folder after folder.

"Fine," Eddie said as he turned toward the door. "I'll ask."

"What are you going to ask for?"

Eddie stopped and gnashed his teeth before turning around. "I guess I don't know. Why don't you tell me, all-knowing master? Why are we in this giant, dusty closet while a seventeen-year-old girl is still out there missing?"

Donald pulled an opened dark green folder out of the box, bolting up out of his chair so fast that it was sent sliding back toward the wall. Eddie could see that his partner's eyes were wide, and there was even the hint of a smile on his perpetually downturned lips.

"Substance." Donald flipped the folder around so Eddie could see the form that captured his attention. There was a small note attached to it.

Eddie squinted in the low light of the room so he could read the typed words. "As stipulated in Trust Instrument 93-KRFT, occupancy by eligible lineal descendant satisfies residency requirement for referred inheritance clause. Verified by legal counsel—see addendum 93-KRFT-1B for confirmation of 12-month requirement." Feeling like he was going cross-eyed, he blinked and shook his head. "What the hell am I reading, man?"

"That is a trust that was legally filed two years ago," Donald explained, pointing to the top of the memo. "See that 93 there? That's the year. These legal files abbreviate last names to four letters, so Kraft is the KRFT."

An inheritance, Eddie thought. "Residency requirement. So, someone filed a trust that would bring the Krafts back to Ransom Creek..."

"Where there just so happens to be affordable housing options for a single mother," Donald added, flipping through the pages in the folder. "And the addendum was prepared by the legal counsel that represents none other than—"

Together they said, "Marcus Vandrel."

Eddie clapped his hands together. "I knew I didn't like the look of that guy at the murder scene. So, where can we find him?"

Donald closed the folder, tucked it under his arm, and closed the box it came from. "We don't." He returned the box to the shelf and added, "We visit the Kraft estate."

Seeing no logic in that move, Eddie just had to scratch his head. "The place is vacant, right? That huge place on the east side?"

Donald strode past him toward the archives' door. "It's currently being managed by a local real estate firm. Which gives the perception that it's being prepped for a sale. There were rumors that the place was going up for auction back in '86 or something, but nothing ever came from it. I guess I always assumed Vandrel had some hand in it. This confirms it," he added, holding up the folder again. "But we're not going to let Marcus know we have it until we can connect it to something concrete."

"Like a missing girl?" Eddie asked, but even as the words came out of his mouth, he knew that they had no rational way to link those things yet.

Donald spun on him then, just before opening the door. He pointed a firm finger into Eddie's chest and narrowed his eyes. "We're onto something here, Rane. And the girl's a part of it. You think we're going to get any closer to finding her by showing our hand to someone that might want her to stay gone?" He moved his finger from Eddie's chest to gesture toward the window. "You think we'll track her down quicker if we're out in the ravine with the uniforms? Sniffing with the dogs?"

Eddie took the point, but only glared at the man making it.

Taking a deep breath and fixing his jacket, Donald said, "We go over and check out the property—see if anyone's been there. If the Kraft girl or Keene have snooped around at all, I'm sure we'll know." He motioned with the folder again. "And maybe we can find out why Marcus is so intent on Victoria Kraft coming home."

Even though he didn't like the way Donald said it, Eddie couldn't argue the logic of the move. So, as Donald strode out of the archives, he followed quietly for a change.

During lunch, Madison skipped the line and went out to the cafeteria tables, frantically looking for Cassandra. She wasn't even sure if she could share this—whatever it was—with her best friend, but she had no one else to go to. Her heart sank when she finally found Cassandra.

She was sitting and chatting with Valerie Collins.

Despite the jealousy Madison harbored over Valerie's apparent relationship with Cliff, there wasn't exactly much animosity between the girls. Still, Madison certainly didn't want to broach the subject of the flushed story in Valerie's presence.

Taking a calming breath, Madison approached the table. "Hey, Cassie."

"Oh, Maddie!" Her friend spun in her seat and motioned for Madison to sit down between her and Valerie. "Come here, listen to this. Val saw Rachel last night!"

Madison's heart lurched. Could it be? Was Rachel back? Did that mean it was actually Rachel pranking her with that damn page describing her crashing the party? In a daze, she sat down, waiting to hear the details.

"I didn't say it was definitely her," Valerie said with an annoyed voice, inspecting a spoonful of yogurt as if it might contain poison. "I'm just saying it was probably her. Just 'cause—how many girls in Ransom Creek have black hair and combat boots? I mean, seriously. Call the fashion police already."

Madison tried to project a calm and collected aura as she asked, "What'd you see?"

Valerie turned toward her. "She rang our doorbell last night. When I went to answer it, she was just standing out there in the dark, on the sidewalk, staring at me like a freak. I swear her eyes were like creepy little cat eyes. All yellow. So, I told her to screw off and slammed the door."

Then, Valerie took the bite of her yogurt and pointed the empty spoon up toward the high cafeteria ceiling. "Then, she threw a basketball or something up on our roof! Freaking psycho!" She went back to scooping more yogurt out of its container.

Madison looked at Cassandra, whose eyes were wide with intrigue. It seemed like Valerie's story had gripped her friend's imagination, which somehow made Madison eager to share her own story with the girls.

"I think it was Rachel," Madison said, looking over her shoulder to make sure no one else was joining their table. When she looked back at Valerie and Cassandra, both girls were staring intently at her.

Then Madison told them everything: the page Elijah found at the murder scene, Rachel banging on the stall door, and how she flushed the evidence.

During the story, Valerie's eyes gradually widened until they were the size of ping pong balls. And then, when Madison finished the tale, she set down her yogurt, spun in her seat, and dug something out of her backpack.

The paper Valerie placed on the table was similar to the one Madison had flushed, but the words were different.

"I found it this morning in my front bushes," Valerie said. "I thought she was still just messing with me...because it's all about the house my mom manages—the old Kraft place."

CHAPTER 12
A BURNING NEED

D ebbie shoved the box off the table, watching its contents spill across the recently vacuumed carpet. Framed pictures, photo albums, and other memorabilia were just about all she found during her search, which wasn't surprising. She had helped pack up most of the estate's heirlooms when Marcus had sourced the property's management to Rose & Collins Real Estate.

But Debbie felt compelled to go through the motions of re-cataloging everything in light of that morning's discovery. If Jonathan had hid some of Walter Kraft's ashes here in the manor... Well, Debbie really had no idea what that would mean for her or the other members of the Remains.

She just knew that Marcus Vandrel was dangerous enough on a normal day—she had no desire to see him backed into a corner while being blackmailed by a dead man.

Thinking about Jonathan made her eyes wander to one of the framed photos on the ground. Debbie cocked her head and leaned forward to get a better look at Caroline Kraft's family in the grainy photo.

Caroline's father, Jeremiah Kraft, wore a three-piece suit, his big 1970s hair neatly combed over and his mustache properly trimmed. Monica Kraft was corpse-like: her long black hair draped on either side of her pale, skull mask of a face. That image took Debbie back to the first time she had ever stepped foot in this damned house, back in the summer of 1973.

"I know what people say." Caroline Kraft was inspecting her nails, as if not wanting to meet Debbie's eyes. She displayed none of the arrogance that she had at school, which made Debbie feel slightly guilty for this whole ruse. "They say my mom's a witch—that this place is cursed."

"People are dumb," Debbie said, rocking in the big chair as she marveled at the high ceiling. She had never been in such a big house. Even the mansions she saw in movies seemed conservative compared to the notorious Kraft Manor. "I think it was just because of your grandpa—he was pretty weird, right?"

Caroline looked up then, the hint of a smile on her lips. "You gotta be crazy to set yourself on fire I think."

Debbie stopped rocking and leaned toward her. "So it's true?"

From the couch where she sat, Caroline just stared for a moment at her new "friend," as if deciding whether or not she could trust her.

You can't, Debbie thought, but just waited for a response.

"It was an accident," she said finally, looking back at her thumbnail—the cuticle looked red and angry from Caroline's picking at it. "My dad tried to save him, but the bonfire collapsed on the old nutjob."

Unsure of how to respond, Debbie gave a single forced chuckle to test the waters. When Caroline looked up with a grin, they both shared a little laugh over the crazy old man's demise.

Debbie suspected it was the perfect time to broach the subject now. She leaned farther forward in the big rocker and glanced at the foyer, even though there had been no indication of the elder Krafts coming home (and little Victoria was already in bed snoozing).

"You know, people around here also say that your grandpa was in a cult..."

"No, he wasn't," Caroline replied, as if expecting the subject to come up. "He was just insane. Worshipped something called Adratheon—which I think has something to do with a cult, but not one he was part of." She stood up and walked toward the mantel above the fireplace. The moonlight came in from the high windows and, mixed with the low, flickering light of the fire, Caroline seemed to glow. "He was just nuts and tried to kill my dad."

The flames in the fireplace lashed out then, and Debbie saw a hand reach out toward Caroline. She gasped and recoiled just when—

—the doorbell rang, startling Debbie out of the memory. She stood up from the desk that was now covered in Kraft memorabilia and walked toward the stairs, making an effort to avoid the den so she wouldn't have to relive the rest of that memory.

Opening the front door, Debbie was greeted by an empty porch. She stepped outside and looked around the long drive. Marcus' car was obviously gone and her own vehicle sat alone.

"Hello? Is somebody there?" She tried to sound professional and inviting—never knew when a buyer was near—but the uncertain fear rising within her made the words sound jagged and accusatory.

She waited a moment to hear footsteps or shuffling, but the only sound came from the birds above or the occasional car in the distance.

And paper rustling.

Debbie turned toward that noise and saw a piece of paper neatly tucked under a rock on the porch. It was just flapping innocently in the breeze, but to Debbie it was a serpent's tongue beckoning her back into the house.

There was no question in Debbie's mind that it was another page from Jon's book, but there were plenty of questions concerning how it had gotten there. Did Marcus leave it as some sort of warning? Why wouldn't he have just given it to her, like the other one?

She wouldn't put such games past Marcus Vandrel, but the man's demeanor that morning did not suggest he was in the mood for subtlety.

After a long moment of dread, Debbie finally walked over and snatched the paper. She took a deep breath before she flipped it over and read the words.

Each paragraph was a finger of seared flesh wrapping itself slowly around her heart, squeezing.

"She's gonna know," Debbie told me at school that day. "We haven't even talked since middle school. She'll know I'm messing with her."

I assured her she was being paranoid. Caroline Kraft had no friends. She would be thrilled if one of the most popular girls at Valley High wanted to suddenly be her friend.

"Why are we even doing this?" Debbie asked, despite my convincing arguments. "Do you really believe Marcus? That Walter Kraft actually cursed his own granddaughter?"

I wanted to laugh in her face, despite how much I actually loved her. She made it sound like it was some kind of choice. As if she hadn't been there when the Remains bore witness to Adratheon's power beneath the lodge.

Each of us was now Marcus' prisoner in that cult, and the repudiation of his power was the only key that would set us free. Which is why we would never escape that prison.

I'm still there, writing this memoir about how we murdered an innocent girl.

Debbie sucked in a ragged gasp as she wadded the paper up, clutching it to her chest as if she could somehow bury into her heart where the true memory had been kept these past twenty years.

"That son of a bitch," she breathed, walking back inside and slamming the front door. But almost immediately, the doorbell rang again.

This time Debbie shrieked, spinning around to see the silhouette of a young girl through the distorted glass of the door. She stood frozen, looking at Caroline Kraft's ghost.

It couldn't be. But it was. Even through the distorted shapes of the door's window design, there was no mistaking Caroline's black hair—darker than the consuming nightmares that still haunted Deborah Collins.

"No," she said, her voice a creaking whisper. "You're dead."

The shape beyond the front door didn't move, but the bell sounded again, once more jolting Debbie. This time she didn't scream, but she began backing away from the door until she was pressed up against the wall dividing the main hall from the den to her left.

That was when the fireplace blazed to life. It was a quiet *fwoosh* sound, which, under normal circumstances, would have been a pleasant surprise, but now almost gave Debbie a heart attack.

She jerked her head in either direction, making sure no one else was in the house. There were exactly three other ways into the place: the sliding back door (which was bolted and secured with a locking bar), the garage entry (which was also bolted, and the overhead doors were turned off), and basement access (which she had sealed).

Unless someone snuck in while she had left the front door open, but that seemed very unlikely.

The doorbell rang again, but Debbie almost anticipated it now. She just turned slowly from the fire back to the front door to find the sunlight twinkling through the distorted glass, no longer obscured by the shape of a dead girl.

Debbie exhaled carefully. The wadded-up paper was still clutched to her chest. Not knowing why, she felt the sudden need to burn the thing, as if the fire was her cue to rid the world of Jon's final betrayal.

She crossed the dreaded den—it was the one room in the house she avoided at all costs, as it was the setting for the most vile act she had ever carried out. Even though the distance from the foyer to the fireplace mantel was probably less than thirty feet, time slowed to a crawl when Debbie's eyes met the ominous image of Walter Kraft.

Time slowed so much that it receded by twenty-one years once more...

Debbie's seventeen-year-old eyes widened as she stared at the old photo of the former Kraft patriarch. "What happened?"

"I'm sure you've heard," Caroline replied, staring into the fire. "He killed himself, after trying to kill my dad."

Nervously, Debbie watched the Kraft girl, unsure if she should push further than she already had. But she had to know—before she let the Remains have their way with her, she had to know for sure.

"He actually burned himself at the stake?"

Caroline laughed. She actually laughed, as if Debbie had just told a joke. "It wasn't like the witch trials or something. There was no stake. He just threw himself on the bonfire. Tried to burn all the family's money, but my dad managed to salvage some of it."

It was true, Debbie thought, *just like Marcus said during her initiation. The old nut wanted to curse his entire bloodline for not following the faith.* Debbie had felt the breath of Adratheon herself that night in the basement of the lodge, and she somehow knew that Walter Kraft had fed himself to the dragon's flames, even before this confirmation.

And yet, hearing it now from Caroline's own lips... "You were there," Debbie said, turning her gaze from the eternal stillness of Walter Kraft to rest upon his scion. "You saw it happen, didn't you?"

Before Caroline could answer, the front door rattled opened and Jeremiah's voice carried in from the foyer. "...don't believe it! There's no way we overdrafted again."

"It's fine, Jere," Mrs. Kraft consoled timidly. "I don't like those people anyway. We don't need to be members there."

"That's not the point, Monica! It means the account's frozen again. Six years dead and the old bastard is still cursing me from the grave!"

"Jeremiah!" The rest of Monica's reply was lost as Caroline grabbed Debbie's arm, dragging her away from the fireplace and out of the den.

"Let's go out back," Caroline said. There was a playfulness in her voice that countered the argument brewing in the other room in a way that unsettled Debbie. The wild look in Caroline's eyes only exacerbated the realization that allowed Debbie to carry out the deceit:

The realization that Caroline Kraft was crazy.

"You knew why you brought me there."

Debbie spun to face Caroline Kraft—the eighteen-year-old dead girl who had just stepped out of her memories. Her long black hair framed a pale face with dark abyssal eyes that bore into Debbie's.

"I was a sacrifice," the corpse girl said.

"No!" Debbie said, backing up toward the fire. "Jonathan said we could just use you—to trick Marcus. We wanted to prove the whole thing was a sham!"

She took another step back. The heat from the fire was almost welcoming in the presence of such icy contempt. But Caroline didn't move. She just stood there, dark eyes narrowed on one of her murderers.

"I didn't know!" Debbie was shrieking now, not just out of fear but because the fire was actually burning her as she continued to try to distance herself from Caroline. "I had never seen Marcus do something like that! Those hands!"

As if the words themselves were the incantation, smoky black claws took shape on either side of Caroline. Those crooked fingers that once strangled the life from Caroline Kraft now reached for Deborah Collins.

Screaming in terror, Debbie threw herself away from those forms that had invaded her nightmares for the past twenty years and fell into the hungry flames.

Rachel Kraft stood unmoving and unblinking as the crazy woman thrashed in the fire. Her screams were inhuman, but they couldn't break through the catatonic state that locked the girl in place.

All she could was watch as the man in the coat stepped around her. He grabbed an iron rod from next to the fire and used it to pin the struggling woman in the fire until finally she stopped screaming and thrashing.

Those black hands enveloped Rachel then, and she disappeared from Ransom Creek once again.

CHAPTER 13
WHAT REMAINS

Sweating, Roger struggled to get his jacket off as he raced toward his office where the phone was ringing. His assistant Brittany opened her mouth to tell him something, but Roger waved his free hand in a dismissive gesture. With his other arm free, he shut his door and hurried around to his chair to answer the phone by the next ring.

"Sorry, Lydia," he said, panting. He wiped sweat from his brow. "Had a couple logs to throw onto the fire."

"It's fucking August, Roger. Just let it die."

He shook his head and didn't bother explaining his figure of speech. If Rothen knew what was happening in Ransom Creek, they would start rethinking their expansion, so the less he said right now the better.

Fortunately, Lydia Thompkins was as impatient as ever. "Please tell me you've made some progress. The team broke ground on the facility's next level last week and we will need some official cover."

"Y-yes," Roger stammered, buying himself some time. He couldn't outright lie to the Rothen Corporation and say that he got Marcus on board with the plans, but he had at least finally gotten him to agree to a meeting—even though it was postponed by a murder. "He's interested. I should be able to finalize something this weekend. Windsor can expedite things from there."

There was a slight pause on the other end before Lydia's cold voice asked, "So you haven't gotten a firm agreement yet?"

A bead of sweat trickled down the side of Roger's temple and stung the corner of his eye. "No," he had to admit.

Instead of the outburst he expected, Lydia took a deep breath. "You're leaving me no choice, Roger. I'm going to have to send a team out there. We cannot leave the site exposed like this."

Roger took off his glasses and wiped his damp face with his sleeve. "That's a bad idea, Lydia. If anyone sees the Rothen Corps out there, it's going to jeopardize all of this. Marcus barely got the council to approve his little trailer park. Can you imagine how they're going to react if they know a goddamn secret lab is going in under the new lodge?"

Her voice remained surprisingly collected. "I'm not a moron, Roger. I wouldn't send the Corps. We have a more...off-the-books team for these sorts of things. They aren't the sort you want hanging around your town for long though, so you better resolve this situation sooner rather than later."

Roger was imagining the headache he would have trying to explain this to Patrick—a man he dreaded encountering even on a good day.

"And that's not the only short fuse you're dealing with, Dupree."

He opened his eyes then, as if Lydia had just dropped a sack of flaming shit on his desk. "What do you mean?"

"Your friend Mr. Vandrel may not have control of his own company much longer."

Something thorny wormed its way up through Roger's bowels. A sudden memory flashed through his mind in that brief, excruciating silence.

Jonthan Keene lowered his hood. The flickering candlelight permanent-
ly etched the lines of the young writer's face into Roger's mind: his large
nose, those sunken eyes that somehow *saw* everything, and his lips that
seemed to only smirk with unchallenged arrogance.

"You look scared, man."

Roger lowered his own hood, watching the other figures turn down
the hall toward the basement's stairs. "Why the hell aren't you scared?!
You saw what I just saw, right?!"

Jonathan pulled the robe over his head, revealing the plaid, tweed
jacket that always made him look ten years older than anyone else at
school. "We see what we're convinced to see."

Pulling off his own robe, Roger moved to look Jonathan in the eyes.
"You're saying I just imagined that?! That Marcus just waved his arms
and we both just separately saw—I don't even know what it was we just
saw, man!"

"Does it matter?" Jonathan turned to follow the rest of the Remains,
but Roger caught his shoulder and turned him back around.

"I don't get it, Jon. You were the most skeptical of all of us—you tried
to convince me not to even join..." Roger motioned to the four-foot
statue of the dragon surrounded by candles, "...all of this. How are you
so...unaffected?"

The smile on Jonathan's face was what would go on to haunt Roger's
restless nights. He often felt guilty for not dreaming more of Caroline
Kraft in her final moments, as she begged for them to rescue her from

the grip of that malevolent thing the Remains had summoned. But it was Jonathan's hollow grin that lurked in the darkest dreams of Roger Dupree.

"I've been numb to this place most of my life," Jonathan said, more with his eyes than his voice. "Marcus promised us fortune—*through the affliction of others do his followers succeed*, right? I don't see any other escape from Ransom Creek except through whatever god-thing's malice we can awaken, and for the first time I see that our leader might not be completely full of shit."

Roger remembered the young writer's laughter then, soft as the distant thunder.

"Unaffected?" Jonathan fixed his jacket and gazed back at the last member to join the Remains. "Roger, this is the most affected I've ever been. For once, I can see beyond the ravine, so say whatever words Marcus tells us to and we'll leech the fortunes from whoever he wants us to curse."

Jonathan took a few steps down the hall before he looked back over his shoulder at Roger and added, "Just don't let him realize that we'll be the ones to decide who gets cursed."

"Are you listening, Roger?"

"Wh—I mean, yes. Of course. What do you mean? About Marcus?"

There was a pointed sigh on the other end of the line. "The Vandrel Group's board of trustees, Roger. Marcus is going to be voted out, so you'll need to make sure he agrees to your proposal before the Cranes take control of the Vandrel holdings."

The sentence took a moment to register in Roger's mind, which was still recovering from the sudden flashback to the basement of the lodge in 1973. Marcus would never give up his family's holding in their company. Not unless...

"Wait." Roger leaned forward, elbows on his desk, as if Rothen's top executive was sitting right across from him. His voice was low. "Are you telling me Marcus Vandrel is broke?"

Patrick Larson picked something out of his teeth as he examined the stitched-up cadaver of Jonathan Keene. He'd lost count of the number of dead bodies he'd seen in this sterile, heartless room, and that fact had given him a strange immunity to mortality; he was unbothered by the concept altogether.

The sheriff flicked whatever he had dug out of his mouth and crossed his arms. "What do we got, Chris?"

The coroner, Chris Herman, was a thin man who had a penchant for hunching. He looked up from his clipboard and leaned on the metal slab where Jonathan took his final rest. "It's like you suspected, Pat. Strangulation. The bruising your deputies pointed out was what did him in. Looks like it was a big guy...almost wrenched the entire head off."

"I know how he died," Patrick said, waving his hand to urge Chris to get to the good stuff. "You said you found something, right?"

"Maybe," Chris said, setting his clipboard down next to Jonathan's lifeless head. As the coroner moved toward his desk, Patrick found himself staring into the sunken eyelids of the man who once made him laugh so hard.

Jonathan Keene was the one who introduced Patrick to his wife, Gabby, back when they were all in eighth grade together. Even though Patrick was a star quarterback and could have had his pick of any of the girls in school, something about Gabby had bewitched him and he would settle for no one else.

It was Jonathan who had broken the ice for him, since Gabby had been such a bookworm. He took Patrick to the Ransom Public Library on the same day he knew she would be there, and he instigated a conversation about some author that Patrick had never even heard of.

Staring at the corpse now, Patrick's eye twitched and he felt the need to rub it suddenly.

"It's the weirdest thing," Chris said, drawing the sheriff's gaze away from the body. "That burn pit where the body was found would account for the ashes, but I put some of the substance found along the subject's—I mean, Mr. Keene's neck under the microscope, and...well..."

"Well what?"

Chris straightened, making him look much taller than Patrick had ever realized. "Well, usually when someone spreads the ashes of a loved one, my guess is those ashes wouldn't be concentrated enough for anyone to really notice. So either Jonathan was tending to someone's final rites, or he interrupted someone else in the process."

Patrick narrowed his eyes, looking to the corpse and then back to Chris. "What are you saying, Herman? Spell it out."

"I'm saying whoever strangled him had human remains covering their hands."

CHAPTER 14
A TRAIL OF RUIN

E ddie's tapping on the car door was even getting on his nerves now, but it really felt like they may be onto something. He could hear Donald's teeth grinding; somehow he didn't feel that bad about it.

As they pulled up to the notorious Kraft Manor, Eddie whistled. "Place really stands out around here."

Donald pulled the car to a stop. There was another car in the carriage loop, so they parked along the curb and walked up the winding way to the porch.

"So how long since someone's lived here?" Eddie asked.

"Almost twenty years," Donald replied immediately, as if expecting the question. "Before Victoria returned, there were no Krafts remaining in Ransom Creek. Walter Kraft had very specific instructions in his will that only a Kraft could ever own this property. It's been managed by the city since his son, Jeremiah, died—same year as Caroline, actually..."

"Seems way too nice a place to just sit here and rot away," Eddie remarked, admiring just how well-maintained the place actually looked up close. "Whoever is managing the property is doing a great job at least."

"It's Deborah Collins—yet another known associate of Marcus Vandrel."

Eddie stopped walking, staring at Donald. "So, this property that's set to be inherited by our missing girl—who seems to only be back in town because of Vandrel and his connection with that city planner—is managed by another one of his inner circle?"

Donald stopped, turning slowly to regard the manor and then his partner. Eddie could tell that laying it all out aloud definitely refocused Donald's thoughts.

"You're right. We should bring Vandrel in after this—there's too much leading back to him."

Eddie just nodded, glad to hear that they might be on the same page finally. "Let's go check—"

Before he finished, a purple Volkswagen Beetle pulled swiftly up the drive and pulled to such a sudden stop that its tires squealed.

"What the hell is she doing out of school?" Donald strode toward the car. Eddie couldn't see who drove due to the glare on the windshield, so he followed out of sheer curiosity—which was quickly sated.

"Dad?!" Madison Avery exited the passenger side of the car, looking both sullen and shocked. "Why are you here?"

"I'd ask you the same thing." Donald assumed the classic disapproving dad pose: hands on hips, legs spread wide, head cocked ever so slightly forward so he could rain judgement down. "I don't remember hearing about a half day…"

"It's my fault, Mr. Avery."

Eddie saw an absolutely breathtaking girl emerge from the driver's side. She had blonde curls and just enough makeup to look ten years older than she should.

The new girl motioned to Madison. "I asked her to come with me. I had a girl-thing-situation and needed to come see my mom—she wasn't answering the home line, so I figured she'd be here." She pointed toward the parked car.

Eddie smiled at that, remembering how much he had wished he had a vagina during high school—periods always seemed like the perfect excuse for cutting class.

Donald didn't reply; from behind him, Eddie couldn't be sure, but he assumed his partner was staring at his daughter to see if she was lying. Unable to bear the strange encounter, Eddie stepped forward.

"Well, how about you go have a word with her first. We were actually here to ask her a few things about her work."

A third girl emerged from the back passenger side, further convincing Eddie that this "girl's problem" was bullshit.

"Valerie, you go ahead," Donald said. "Madison. Cassandra. You can both wait out here with us."

Valerie hesitated for a moment, but then gave a curt nod and hurried toward the gigantic porch.

Eddie was so uncomfortable with his remaining company that he rested a hand on his gun as he turned away from whatever it was Donald was whispering to his daughter. He had only had to draw his weapon with intention seven times while on the job, and only three of those times did he have to discharge it. However, he still found a strange reassurance from merely touching the weapon, as if it reminded him of both his capabilities and his capacity for restraint.

"Mom! What's that smell?"

Valerie's voice carried across the drive, and Eddie thought he caught a whiff of something just as the girl shrieked.

Drawing his gun, Eddie first made sure Donald had the other girls covered before he rushed toward the front door. The smell reminded him of a killer barbeque place he used to hang out at back in Charlotte. But when he caught sight of the source, he almost threw up. Memories of Kevin Blankenship slathering up ribs with his homemade sauce were forever ruined by what he now saw.

A woman's legs were sticking out of a blazing fireplace, the limbs contorted in grotesque positions. One of her stylish pumps was kicked off a few feet away while the other one had melted to become part of her blackened appendage.

"You fucking psycho witch!" Valerie screamed, jerking Eddie's attention from the burning corpse to another figure in the room. As if the scene weren't already bizarre enough, Eddie had to blink several times to make sure he saw what he thought he saw.

The figure holding Valerie's attention was a young girl, probably the same age. She had dark hair framing a pale, slack face—the girl's gaze was transfixed on the fire. She hadn't even heard Valerie's deafening screams.

"I'm going to fucking kill you!"

Even as Valerie flew toward the girl with her fingers curled into vicious claws, the only witness to this heinous act did not visibly respond—she just stared into the satiated flames.

Eddie's reflexes were compromised in the current situation, and he wasn't able to stop Valerie from tackling the other girl. However, Donald had followed him inside and was between the girls before much damage was done. Eddie went closer to the fire to see if he could put it out, but he felt his lunch coming up as he saw the true horror that the fireplace contained.

"Don't, Rane! Go call it in!"

Eddie turned to do so, but before he got far he heard Donald's voice catch in his throat.

"Jesus Christ, Eddie. It's Rachel Kraft."

As Madison watched the police and the paramedics do their practiced dance, she thought of all the times she had interacted with Mrs. Collins. The woman wasn't the warmest person—not lively and jovial like Mrs. Dupree, who acted like one of her girlfriends—but she was always nice to Madison. Thinking of her burning in a fireplace was just too much for her to fully process at the moment.

So she just distracted her mind by guessing what each person's job was at the crime scene.

"Do you think she did it?"

Madison turned to Cassandra, who sat next to her in back of the ambulance. Neither of them were hurt, but her dad told them to stay there until he got done inside the house (where they were certainly not allowed to go).

Cassandra nodded toward the house. "You heard Valerie in there. It had to be Rachel, right?"

Madison didn't want to consider it. Whatever happened in that house, it was clear to her that Valerie's mom was dead—how she had died must have been too terrible to even describe, because her dad didn't even try.

"You can't tell him," Cassandra said. And when Madison looked at her again, the girl gave her a pointed and urgent stare. "If your dad knew what Valerie did at lunch on Friday...we could get blamed for this, Maddie!" Her eyes darted toward the house, probably making sure that nobody had heard the panicked voice. "Let's just pretend we don't know anything...let Valerie do the talking."

"Madison!"

Her dad's voice startled her, and she bolted to her feet. He motioned for her to come to the porch. Madison gave Cassandra a discreet nod of agreement and went to her dad.

"I'm sorry about your friend's mom, Maddie."

While Madison was glad he was sympathetic and not mad at her, something about her dad's voice unsettled her. She never witnessed him talking to a criminal or doing serious police work, but she imagined this was what he sounded like. There was a danger to the gentle, controlled way his voice sounded.

"What happened, Dad?"

Looking over his shoulder at his new partner, who was talking to one of the other cops, her dad just took a deep breath and said, "It's bad, hon. We found your friend Rachel, but she's...I guess, catatonic they said."

Peering around her father's shoulder, Madison caught a glimpse of Rachel in the house. She was sitting in a chair, staring at the ground blankly. She didn't move at all while the paramedics inspected her.

"What does that mean?" Madison wanted to focus the conversation on Rachel or Mrs. Collins, and not Valerie or what happened at school on Friday last week.

"It just means that she's gone through something very traumatic and isn't ready to deal with it yet—she's just completely unresponsive. So they're going to take her to the hospital and keep her under observation while we try to figure out what happened here."

Madison felt tears coming. She always knew she loved her parents, but having her dad here taking care of this awful situation... She didn't feel it was fair hiding things from him. But she was just too scared. "I'm sorry, Dad..."

Her father's eyes softened then. "Sorry for what, Maddie? You had nothing to do with this—how could you have known?"

She hugged him then, harder than she ever remembered hugging him or Mom. But she felt apprehension when he laid a hand on her shoulder.

"Why did you and your friends come here?"

Madison stiffened, her mind racing for rational excuses. But she felt like her dad hadn't even remotely believed the period story Valerie tried to use. Fortunately, Detective Eddie Rane saved the day.

"Don!"

Her dad patted her shoulder gently and said, "We'll talk back at the station. Go back with Cassie and wait for us, alright? You don't want to see any of this."

Madison walked miserably back to the ambulance, fearing any further discussions. However, her mind was also wrestling with how she could get into that house and see if there were any other pages that might explain the nature of Rachel Kraft.

"Sheriff, we got this under control."

Patrick gave the new detective a withering glare, not truly believing he heard the man right. "What's that, Detective Rane?"

"I said we got this under control." His smile was absolutely villainous. "Our missing person was here, so we'll follow up and brief your team on what we find."

"Like hell you will, Rane." Patrick struggled to maintain his composure as he marched toward the insolent prick. "What's this, your second day here? You have any idea who you're talking to?"

"We do."

Patrick turned around to glare at Donald Avery now. The man had his arms crossed over his splendid blue suit.

"You know how things work around here, Avery. We have a homicide in a residence that's technically the property of the city, and you're going to try to block me? You want to take this to the fucking mayor?"

Patrick got a little hard from the sour look that crossed Donald Avery's face then, but the expression was gone quickly and replaced by a stern scowl.

"Sure, Pat. Take it up with the mayor. Tell him we had a missing person show up next to a dead body and see what he thinks of those optics...changing hands mid-investigation."

"Excuse us."

Patrick turned around to see the coroners pushing the body bag on a stretcher, needing to pass by where the three cops were arguing in the foyer.

"Don't worry," Eddie Rane said. "I take very good notes, Sheriff. You can follow up after we finish our investigation."

Patrick Larson, for the first time since he could ever remember, felt powerless.

CHAPTER 15
ANSWERS

Roger was almost grateful for the bizarre turn of events.

As he strode past the young woman greeting him in the police department's lobby, he thought of how just yesterday he was tempted to go to the police about Jonathan's murder, not knowing what he'd tell them. Now, his daughter was being questioned about a different murder, and that shifted the focus from his plight.

He no longer felt like he was under scrutiny, and it was his job as a father and protector to demand why Cassandra was being questioned by the police.

"Mr. Dupree," the woman was calling after him, but Roger didn't slow down.

"Where's my daughter?" Roger asked no one in particular. "Cassie!"

"Daddy!"

Her voice came from a closed door at the end of the hall. Roger could see Donald Avery through the door's window, but his new partner was the one that opened the door.

"Mr. Dupree," he said, scratching his thick mustache with one of his fingers. "Can I have a quick word?"

"Not until I see my daughter," Roger snapped, trying to move past the man. But the guy didn't move, not even when Roger's chest collided with his shoulder—which was surprisingly sturdy, even though the detective didn't look much bigger than him.

"She's not being questioned or anything," the detective said. "I'm not sure if you remember me from yesterday, but my name is Detective Eddie Rane, and your daughter's friend saw something terrible this afternoon. My partner is just explaining the process to your daughter. Do you mind if I brief you on the situation?"

Roger peered around Eddie to see his daughter sitting next to her friend Madison. Cassandra gave him a nod to indicate that she was alright.

"What happened?" Roger asked, allowing Eddie to lead him to the empty room across the hall. "They wouldn't tell me anything over the phone except that Cassie and her friends were at a crime scene."

"I understand you're an acquaintance of Deborah Collins?"

No, Roger thought, knowing exactly what was coming. First Jonathan and now Debbie. Roger had been completely in love with Debbie since the third grade, but she was obsessed with Jonathan—the mysterious writer that seemed to draw schoolgirls like rockstars drew groupies.

Now they were both dead.

"I'm sorry to say—"

"How?" Roger interrupted. "Was it the same person who killed Jonathan?" He almost said the name Marcus Vandrel and had to catch himself. In his mind, it seemed most likely that Marcus was the killer; the fact that the man was broke made Roger even more certain that Marcus would do anything to avoid his secrets getting out.

"We can't say for sure yet," the detective replied. "That's why we would like to question your daughter, if you would be willing to sit with us."

"Did she see something?"

The detective looked away for a moment, giving the impression that he didn't believe so, but he just said, "That's what we want to find out."

"Sure," Roger said, turning toward the room was daughter in. He ran a hand over his balding scalp.

"Can I ask you something real quick?"

Roger turned back to Eddie. The detective leaned in toward him, his eyes glancing toward the closed door across the hall before returning to Roger's. "Have any of your employees at the lodge mentioned seeing anything...strange this past weekend?"

Roger's thoughts were scrambling, but he managed to maintain a stern expression. "Perhaps we can discuss that after I tend to my daughter, Detective?"

Eddie held his gaze for a long moment before smiling. "Of course. I look forward to that discussion."

Back in the room with the girls, Roger sat next to Cassandra and briefly consoled her before Donald took the seat across the table from them. Roger noted that the man's own daughter was on his side of the table, as if they were all subject to Donald Avery's scrutiny.

Eddie shut the door before crossing his arms and leaning against it. "We've explained to the girls what happened to Mrs. Collins—a horrible situation, and something her daughter never should have seen."

"Perhaps you could tell me then," Roger replied.

Donald explained that they had found Deborah's body in the fireplace at Kraft manor. Cassandra sobbed under Roger's comforting arm, but his mind was years—no, decades away. As the detectives shared details about the murder scene, Roger replayed a memory in his mind from the worst night of his life.

In 1974, there wasn't a whole lot to do in Ransom Creek. There was a nice movie theater, but Roger didn't really enjoy sitting in dark, crowded rooms. The soda fountain, called Duke's Candy Bar back then, was alright, but anyone hanging out there over the age of thirteen was viewed with social disdain in high school.

So, Sycamore Hollow was where he and his friends spent the majority of their free time. And that continued after Marcus convinced them to start their little club.

"It's a cult," Jonathan had told him the night before. "I mean, let's call a spade a spade, right? We all might not truly be worshipping the dark powers that Marcus believes in, but we're certainly united for a malign cause."

"Malign?" Roger glanced at him from the driver's seat, careful not to take his eyes too far from the road. He hated how the guy always tried to use big words that no one understood. "What the hell's that supposed to mean?"

Jonathan laughed, reaching for the cigarette lighter that just popped. As he lit his smoke and rolled down the window to let the summer breeze in, he replaced the lighter and just said, "It means we're playing with fire, Rodge-baby. We might as well just be straight about it."

But despite Jonathan's brash attitude, he kept the Remains a secret, just like the rest of them. And when the night came, he played his part.

The night in question was a Sunday—the last Sunday of school. They had lured Caroline Kraft to the ravine under the pretense that they were having a graduation party for all the seniors. A party with a bonfire at the very site where Walter Kraft had burned alive; but they left that last little tidbit out.

They wore their robes to begin the ceremony. It was a sacred rite that Marcus had read about from his family's personal records. Roger felt a little silly reciting the praises to Adratheon, but he would be lying if he didn't say it made him feel...integral.

When they were done with the ceremony, Roger was the first one to remove his ceremonial garb. Jonathan's words from the night before still bothered him. He supposed he didn't have a problem with being in a cult if it meant he might be able to avoid the same fate as his father: tied to the pressures of appeasing others just so he could afford the lifestyle he felt he deserved.

"Is Debbie going to come through?" Benjamin asked, shoving his own robe into his bag. "She seemed to have a little hesitation... Think she's got a bit of a soft spot for these Krafts?"

"She'll get her here," Jonathan assured him. "Just worry about your pronunciation, Ben. Every time you say Adratheon it sounds like Ah-dray-thee-on. Put your balls into it, man." He assumed a strong pose and bellowed, "Ah-draaahh-thay-on!"

"That doesn't matter," Marcus snapped, serious as always. "Just make sure when she gets here we all say it together. If this is really where her grandfather did it, then the offering will be complete."

Roger looked down at the burn pit, still feeling uneasy knowing that Walter Kraft's ashes had just appeared as if from nowhere. Of course, it was perfectly realistic to suspect that Marcus had brought any old ashes in and claimed that they were actually Walter's, but somehow Roger did truly believe all of this was actually happening.

It all just felt too right.

"So do the ashes even matter?" Jonathan asked, as if reading Roger's thoughts. "Does she actually need to see them or anything?"

"Of course they matter," Marcus said. "This kind of power requires a show of faith and devotion—we have to complete the circle that Jeremiah Kraft left unfinished. His daughter is as critical as his father's remains."

Roger looked at Jonathan, suddenly suspicious why he would ask that. He thought of the doubt and skepticism that Jonathan had displayed toward the Remains and what they were trying to do. Roger couldn't help but wonder now if the guy was trying to undermine things or otherwise subvert the members' convictions.

He didn't have much time to dwell on that because Patrick, who had gone up the hill to ensure they were truly alone, came back down shouting, "They're coming! Deb's car just pulled up."

Marcus motioned toward Benjamin. "Get the cooler. And everyone act natural."

Those instructions had the opposite effect on Roger, and now he felt more nervous than ever. His throat was tightening and he had the sudden urge to shit. He heard Patrick descending the hill behind him but his eyes were fixed on Jonathan, who looked less detached than normal—his eyes were fixed on the pile of ashes.

"Roger," Patrick said from behind him. "You good?"

Roger wasn't, but he couldn't seem to pull his eyes from Jonathan. It was as if he sensed something terrible was about to happen and no one else but Jonathan Keene knew.

"Roger?"

Patrick's voice sounded so foreign to him, it was easy to ignore.

"Roger!"

The ravine faded away.

"Roger? Do you understand?"

Blinking, Roger refocused his gaze on Detective Donald Avery. "Yes, I understand." But he didn't. "Do I need a lawyer or anything?"

Donald gave his partner a look, but quickly returned his gaze to Roger. "We're not interrogating you, Roger. You're of course entitled to a lawyer, but we're just focused on the Kraft girl and why she was there with Mrs. Collins. All we really need at this moment is an account." He nodded to Madison. "I've already taken my daughter's statement, but we need Cassandra's as well."

"I told you," his daughter said, "we weren't even inside. Valerie just said she had to talk to her mom, so we rode along to make sure she was alright."

"Do you think she was alright?" Roger turned to Eddie Rane, who still leaned arrogantly against the door and said, "She seemed convinced that Rachel Kraft somehow did that to her mom. Do you know why she'd think that?"

Both girls were silent and exchanged a nervous look before Cassandra said, "I mean, she was alone in there with her."

Donald leaned over the table slightly, resting both elbows atop it. "I know it was a truly terrible thing that your friend experienced. We can't be sure what any of us would do in that situation. But our job is to try as hard as we can to understand why someone would do something. And right now we're trying to understand why your friend would immediately attack Rachel Kraft." He looked from his own daughter to Roger's. "Do you know of any reason why Valerie would think that Rachel would hurt her mom?"

Roger was so busy watching the detectives that he didn't see the look on his daughter's face. But Avery and Rane must have seen something; they exchanged a subtle look. Roger could tell his daughter knew something, and he got to his feet to put an end to this.

"Enough!" Roger pointed at Donald, assuming his most offended and indignant presence. "You can interrogate your own daughter all you want, but I'm not going to let you grill mine after she just went through something like this. Cassandra, get your things, we're leaving." He looked at Rane. "And the sheriff is going to hear about this. We don't do things like this around here. You should know, Avery. This is just absurd!"

With that, he led his daughter out of the room and wondered if he could even go to Patrick now. With Marcus now murdering members of the Remains to cover his own ass, Roger had no idea who he could trust.

After Eddie left to inform Tori Kraft about the current condition of her daughter, Donald sat with Madison in the vacated room.

"You know it's my job to know when people are lying, Maddie." He got up to take off his jacket, letting her process his words as if she were the sole subject of the investigation.

"What am I lying about?" she asked.

"I'm talking about your friend," Donald said, hanging his jacket on the back of his chair before sitting down again. "Cassie knows something about Rachel, doesn't she? When I asked if something happened between her and Valerie, she was clearly hiding something."

Madison bit her lip, which told Donald everything he needed to know. But he waited, arms crossed and gaze leveled, wanting to see if she'd come clean without his prompting.

After a moment of tense silence, Madison leaned forward and put her hands on the table. She was picking the cuticle on her thumb as she spoke with her eyes downcast. "She was worried that it would get Valerie in trouble."

Donald stayed silent.

Madison sighed and looked up defiantly. "It's so stupid—Valerie just does mean crap like that. Rachel shouldn't have taken it so seriously."

Donald waited.

Finally, Madison told her father why Rachel Kraft may have wanted to hurt Valerie Collins.

"Did you see that fucking new girl?" Valerie wielded her mascara brush like a tiny dagger, pointing to the bathroom door. "Flirting with Cliff like she doesn't know perfectly well his parents would never let him hang out with a goddamn Kraft!"

Madison concentrated on washing her hands while Valerie had her meltdown. It was clear that Valerie was in love with Cliff, just like Madison was, but at least Madison didn't make it so *freaking* obvious.

"She needs to be put in her place," Cassandra said in a voice that Madison almost didn't recognize. Her friend tended to adopt Valerie's nastiness when they hung out, and it always bothered Madison.

"She seems pretty quiet to me," Madison offered. She tossed the wadded-up paper towel in the trash and made to leave. "I think she probably knows her place with how everyone in this school talks about the Krafts."

It was the wrong thing to say.

Valerie lowered her mascara wand, her lashes only half-perfect. She gave Madison a withering glare through the mirror's reflection. "Don't tell me you're defending her, Maddie." She turned to face her directly. "Next thing, you'll be hanging out together. Once that happens, you might as well stop talking to us—your life at Valley will be done as far as we're concerned, right, Cassandra?"

After giving Madison a consoling look, Cassandra shrugged and said, "I—"

"Oh my god!" Valerie dropped her arms in frustrated surrender. "You've *got* to be kidding me! Not you too! Come on, who do you think will be caught dead with you if you start hanging out with a Kraft?"

Madison pulled the bathroom door open. "I guess Cliff Windsor might, since at least he treats her like a human being."

Strangely, even the stunned look on Valerie's face didn't give Madison the satisfaction she had expected. Instead, as she let the door close behind her, she felt a strange sense of shame having said that to Valerie—as if she had unintentionally challenged the girl.

Madison knew better than to challenge someone like Valerie Collins when it came to the social structure at Valley High.

Later at lunch, the feeling of foreboding only deepened for Madison, and she found she couldn't even eat her meal.

"What's wrong?" Cassadra took a loud slurp from her Diet Dr. Pepper. "Cramps?"

Madison shook her head, scanning the cafeteria for anything that might explain the dread she felt. But it was just another lunch at school. The football players were being rowdy at the table behind them, and the dweebs were playing with their dorky Magic cards at the table to the other side of them. Madison and Cassandra sat alone, waiting for Valerie, who always managed to be fashionably late. Since they were alone, Madison felt comfortable confiding in her friend.

"I'm pretty sure my parents are getting divorced."

Cassandra's eyes went wide mid-sip and she lowered her beverage. "Did something happen?"

Madison dropped her hands on the table, startling both of them. "No, that's the problem! My dad hasn't done anything—it's like he's just given up. My mom said they just couldn't make it work, but it's like they're not even trying. Ever since he got that apartment, I never even see him make an effort. I guess he's just fine with it all, you know?"

Cassandra had no profound response. She just frowned and reached out to take Madison's hand. "I'm sorry, Maddie."

"Are you alright?"

Both girls spun in their seats to see Rachel Kraft holding her lunch tray with pale fingers tipped in black nails.

Madison had never been this close to the girl, and looking into her eyes she noticed how dark they were, almost like the pupils were unnaturally large and swallowed any color the rest of the eyes might have had.

But despite how haunting Rachel's gaze may have been, Madison also felt a strange comfort from the way the girl looked at her and she almost couldn't resist answering her.

"It's just my parents," Madison said, and wanting to avoid saying more, she motioned to the chair across from her. "Did you want to sit with us?"

Rachel hesitated for a moment, looking in either direction as if she had already made plans to sit somewhere else. But then she gave a faint smile and set her tray down.

Madison could feel Cassandra's glare, but she just ignored her and focused on Rachel. "Getting used to the place yet?"

She gave Madison another shy grin, revealing just how pretty she was. Madison couldn't help being slightly jealous of the girl; being dark and mysterious and apparently flirting with the only guy at Valley High that really mattered to Madison.

"I guess," Rachel replied. "Haven't really been anywhere in town aside from school and the library."

Madison looked at her food, considering what she was about to do. She knew it was a stupid idea, but the way Valerie behaved earlier in the bathroom and having to deal with her parents...she felt like doing something pretty stupid.

"You should come hang out with us tonight," Madison said to Rachel, giving her a genuine smile. Cassandra immediately suffered a coughing fit.

Before Rachel could respond, another voice from behind them added, "Yes, you absolutely must come and hang out with us."

The three girls turned to see Valerie standing near their table. She had her book bag hanging over one shoulder but she didn't have a lunch tray.

Rachel made a *tsk* sound as she looked back at Madison with a confused look on her face.

"I mean, I would have asked you earlier," Valerie continued, "but we all know what happened when the cool kids asked your aunt to hang out." She pulled something out of her bag and tossed it. Whatever it was, it landed on Rachel's tray and splattered her lunch everywhere.

When Madison saw what the thing was, she gasped and pushed herself away from the table as if the object might lash out at her.

But the noose didn't move, and neither did the girls at the table as a wave of gasps rippled across the lunchroom, followed by a moment of vacuous silence.

Then, someone laughed behind Madison, and that triggered a slew of various reactions from their peers.

Cassandra uttered an, "Oh my god, Valerie!" as she used a napkin to clean food off her shirt.

A twerp from the nerd table said, "Whoa! Collins with the *brutality*!"

Someone else warned Valerie, "Watch out, she's gonna curse you, Valerie!"

It soon became a deafening cacophony. Some teacher or security officer shouted, "What's going on over there?" But that just seemed to rile everyone up even more.

Madison's eyes were fixed on Rachel, feeling powerless to offer the girl any consolation in the wake of such a monstrous act. But the Kraft girl just calmly stood up and walked away, not even looking at Valerie or the noose that lay across her tray like a dead snake.

Valerie sat down with a giggle. "You're so welcome for saving your asses."

Madison was just too stunned to do anything other than gather her things and leave.

Jesus Christ, Donald thought, wondering not for the first time how kids could be so damn cruel to each other.

"So, they didn't interact at all after that?" Donald asked.

"Not that I know of," Madison said, staring into the table, but not finding whatever she was looking for. "Except for at the party."

The door opened. "Seriously, Don! Are you interrogating her?" Laura moved over to embrace their daughter. "Are you alright, hon?"

"It's fine," Madison said, giving Donald a look over Laura's shoulder. "I was just helping Dad with the case."

"I doubt he needs your help," Laura said, glaring at Donald as she began ushering Madison out of the room. "Let's get you home and fed—Oh, I'm so sorry to hear about Deborah."

Laura's voice wavered then. Her shoulders began to hunch forward and Donald knew she was crying. She hadn't been necessarily close with Deborah Collins—at least not to his knowledge—but he supposed this sort of tragedy happening so close can cast relationships in a new light.

"I'm sorry," Donald offered, getting up to move toward his family. But Laura waved a hand, dismissing his efforts.

"It's fine, Don. I just want to get her home. I can't believe this happened. Do you know who could do such a thing?"

"That's what we're going to find out." He put his jacket back on.

Laura gave him a nod. "Please do. Come on, Madison."

"I'll be right there," his daughter said. "I need to get my bag from Dad's desk."

Donald walked her back to the bullpen while Laura waited in the lobby. "I'm sorry again about all this," he said. He meant the murder and everything else her and her friends were wrapped up in, but he was thinking about the divorce at the moment. As she grabbed her bag from his desk, he added, "You've helped a lot, Maddie. Seriously. Thank you for being honest with me."

For a moment, it looked like she was about to bite her lip, but she closed her mouth and looked into his eyes before asking, "Did you need to talk to Mom before we leave?"

He looked in the direction of the lobby before looking back at her. "I don't think there's much else to say..."

She looked at the ground before turning to leave.

CHAPTER 16
ALIBIS

"What do you mean?" Eddie asked with a frown. "She told me she had a shift this afternoon."

"She did," the bartender said, wiping a schooner with a wet rag. "They called me in when she didn't show at eleven. When you find her, tell her she owes me another shift."

Eddie knocked on the bartop and looked at his watch. It was almost five. If the department couldn't reach her at home and she wasn't at work, Eddie had no idea where to begin his search for her.

It was in that moment that he realized just how little he knew of this woman, and that led him to lean on his cop intuition. That opened the doors to him wondering if Tori had been near the Kraft place that morning.

Stop with the wild assumptions, man, he thought to himself as he left the bar. Absorbed in his paranoid thoughts, he collided with another body that was rushing into the establishment.

"Sorry," Eddie began, reaching out to brace whoever it was. "Tori?"

Her pained expression turned to pleasant surprise. "Eddie! What are you doing here?"

"Looking for you, actually." It was then that he noticed the jacket she was wearing, which was only really notable due to how big it looked on her—it certainly couldn't be hers—and the fact that, even though it was overcast, it was still almost seventy degrees.

"Oh, I'm sorry," she said, reaching for the door, "I'm actually super late. Trevor's going to kill me."

"It's about Rachel."

Tori froze mid-step and held his gaze with eyes that Eddie could easily imagine belonging to a cornered animal.

Or maybe someone who had something to hide.

"What is it?" Her voice was more panicked than her expression conveyed, and Eddie realized he was leaving a scared mother wondering if her only child was alive or dead. "Eddie, did you find her?"

"We did," Eddie replied, softening his gaze as much as he could to assure her that nothing was wrong, even though plenty was wrong. "She's not hurt, but she's at the hospital. Tori, she's...in a state of catatonic shock."

Tori didn't react to that. Well, not in the way that Eddie expected at least. Her expression shifted ever so slightly to a look of relief.

"This isn't the first time this has happened, is it, Tori?"

Patrick waited until the end of the day before marching into the police department to confront Chief Burke. The logical part of his mind was being infected by basic survival instincts and he was ready to do everything he could to get Avery and Rane off Debbie's murder case.

"Come on in, Sheriff," Burke called before Patrick could even reach his office door to knock. "Herman just called—assuming you're here about the murder."

Patrick slammed the door shut. "You trying to pull rank with me now?"

Owen held up his hands in surrender. "Pat, we gotta have some boundaries, right? At least the appearance of defined procedures, like you said."

"This is the second murder in less than forty-eight hours!" Patrick felt the rage painting his face red, but he didn't care. He pointed back toward the bullpen. "You got a new detective wet behind the ears on a goddamn homicide that's clearly linked to my murder investigation!"

Burke shook his head. "Rane is hardly a rookie. And I get the emotions here, Pat, I do. But you know as well as I do... I mean, shit, you're about as close as it gets to this one. Didn't you date Deborah back in school?"

Patrick couldn't contain his absolute shocked fury that the chief of police was trying to dictate how he ran his town. He kicked one of the chairs facing Burke's desk out of the way and slammed both his fists down on the chief's paperwork. "This is gonna come back on you, Owen! I make one call to O'Brien and you'll be looking at an early retirement with a prorated pension!"

Chief Burke gave him a look that chilled the molten toxicity pumping from Patrick's heart. "You try that, Sheriff. Call me a skeptic, but I don't think you've banked enough favors with the mayor to waste them on someone like me." He took a calm sip from his coffee mug that was adorned with the words *If Caffeine is a Crime, Lock Me Up*.

Parick wanted to slap it out of the man's hands, but instead he settled for shoving the man's tidy stacks of papers to the floor as he stormed off to find Marcus Vandrel.

In a dimly lit hospital room, Eddie stood near the window that over-looked the vacant parking lot. They were only on the second floor, but in a town built as low as Ransom Creek, he had a decent view of the place. It oddly felt more like home to him now than anywhere he had been in the last few years.

Turning to look at Victoria Kraft, who sat next to her currently vacant daughter, he supposed she was mostly to blame for the sense of belonging he was starting to feel.

"How old was she?" Eddie asked, speaking in a low gravelly whisper out of strange consideration for the teenage girl who stared at nothing with wide dark eyes.

"The last time this happened?" Tori didn't shift her gaze from Rachel. "It was about a year ago, I think. Actually...now that I think about it, maybe exactly a year."

Eddie had the urge to jot that down in his notebook, but instead just tried to mentally file it away.

Tori turned toward him. "You said you just found her staring at..." Her voice caught, and she turned back to Rachel. She reached out to take her daughter's limp hand. "What the hell was she doing there?"

Eddie considered his next question very carefully. "Have either of you been there since you moved back?"

"Just once. We had to sign some papers. That was the only time I really interacted with..."

"Deborah Collins." Eddie watched her carefully, to see if the name affected Tori at all.

If it did, she hid it very well.

"I can't believe someone would do that."

Eddie thought of how Valerie had attacked Rachel, the girl fully convinced that her mother had been murdered by her classmate. Even though Eddie couldn't imagine the small Kraft girl overpowering an adult woman and then somehow pinning her into a fireplace without so much as singeing herself in the process, he had to start eliminating any possibility he could; otherwise, all eyes would be on the Krafts for this.

"Did Rachel ever talk to you about anyone at school picking on her? Any bullying, or anything like that?"

Tori pulled her hand back from Rachel, turning to fully face Eddie with a severe look on her face. "Are you asking me as a cop?"

"Tori, you have to understand how this is going to look to people. There are going to be some nasty things being slung around, especially in a small town like this. I want to help. Yeah, I'm a cop, but I'm a cop who wants to help figure out how we can quickly shut down any speculation that your daughter was at that murder scene for any reason other than the wrong place at the wrong time, if you get what I mean."

Eddie was glad to see from Tori's reaction that she did. But it didn't stop her from breaking down and crying.

Cliff Windsor hung up the phone, not entirely sure how to process things. His mom had called to tell him the news, but it didn't feel real. Valerie had just been in his house on Friday complaining about her mom, and now the woman was dead.

Just as he considered picking the phone up and dialing Valerie's number, the doorbell rang and he nearly jumped back like a screaming girl in a slasher movie. Feeling stupid, he went to the stairs to answer, but then whoever was at the door started pounding, making Cliff recoil yet again.

"I'm coming," he shouted. "Jesus!"

Cliff pulled open the door, ready to chastise a solicitor, but when he saw the wealthiest man in Ransom Creek breathing heavily, all he could say was, "Oh. Hi."

"Hey, Clifford," Marcus said between heaving breaths. His eyes darted into the house, searching frantically. "Is your dad home?"

"He should be soon. Is everything alright?"

Marcus looked down at his disheveled appearance and made an effort to adjust his jacket and dress shirt, both of which looked to be missing buttons. "Well, I'm sure you've heard about the awful thing that happened at Kraft manor."

Cliff motioned for him to come in. "Yeah, I just heard. I'm sorry, Mr. Vandrel, I know you were friends with Mrs. Collins."

"Yes..." Marcus' voice sounded very distracted, and he seemed to be looking for something as he paced the entryway.

"You want some water or something while you wait for my dad?"

He turned to Cliff. "Actually, I think I'll just wait for him in his study." Without waiting for permission, Marcus turned and walked down the hall toward the double doors leading to the one room of the huge house that was off limits to everyone except for Benjamin Windsor.

Cliff wondered if he should object, but when the study doors clicked closed he just shrugged and went up to his room to see if he could get ahold of Valerie or Jared.

"My mom told me everything that happened to my sister," Tori explained, having dried her eyes and steadied her breathing. "I was too young to remember much, especially everything that led up to it."

Eddie wanted to ask a hundred questions, but he restrained himself. He had pulled up a chair to sit next to Tori, watching Rachel sleep. The girl's eyes had steadily gotten heavier during their visit, and the nurse said that it was a good sign she was going to sleep; it meant there might be a chance she would wake up normally after enough rest.

"People around here thought Caroline was a witch or something," Tori continued. "Weird stuff happened in town, and it was always somehow a Kraft to blame. But Caroline seemed to get the worst of it after she saw our grandfather die."

Eddie blinked, but tried not to visibly react to the revelation that Rachel, who had just witnessed someone burning alive, had an aunt that witnessed the same thing. He didn't know what that meant, other than it was noteworthy.

"The night she died, my mom told me she was so excited—some kids at school had invited her to a gathering in the ravine. She told Mom she was going to a bonfire."

Eddie's thoughts naturally went back to the dead body he had just seen in the ravine; yet another morbid coincidence. He felt that urge again to question her, but he knew he had to let her get to it on her own time. She was dealing with a lot, and the minute he started pressing, she could easily lock up on him.

"They said she hanged herself in that tree," Tori continued, turning to face Eddie. "Like, she was doing some dare or something—the explanation was total bullshit, and it didn't make any sense. Caroline didn't care what people thought of her. She wouldn't have tried to impress some classmates who hadn't even paid attention to her until our dad died."

Again, it pained Eddie not to ask about her dad, or to not write a note to himself to look into it later, but he fought to just hold her gaze until she was done.

Tori looked back at Rachel. "I hadn't thought about my sister for a long time. Until last year, when..." She reached out and gently took her daughter's hand again.

Eddie waited for almost a minute before he couldn't take it any longer. "What happened last year, Tori?"

"Someone sent a letter to us," she said. "It didn't have an address or anything—like they just slipped it into our mailbox. It was like a page from a book, and Rachel opened it. She read it while I was at work, and when I came home that night she was just sitting on the couch like this, staring at the TV, completely in a trance." She wiped a tear away. "I tried everything: screamed at her, shook her. Eddie, I even slapped her, and I hate myself every day for it, but I had no idea what was wrong." She held her hand up to her mouth as her voice broke again. But she just sniffed and kept going through the emotions. "And I don't even know why I did this, but I took the paper she had been reading, pulled out my lighter, and burned it. I only read some of it while it was on fire, but

I barely remember anything from it...just something about hearing the name Adratheon and obeying... I'll never forget that name, because it was so weird."

This time, Eddie did pull his notebook out, jotting down the name Adratheon and hoping he spelled it right.

Tori watched him but didn't object. "About five minutes after that she was fine. She just blinked a lot and thought she had fallen asleep. Eddie, she didn't even remember reading that thing."

Eddie closed his notebook and tucked it back into his jacket. "Maybe it's better she didn't," he said. He looked at Rachel and hoped she didn't remember today either, even if it meant Deborah Collins' murder went unsolved.

Benjamin parked awkwardly in the drive, not wanting to take the time to reverse his Mercedes and back it up toward the garage properly. Glaring at the fourth page from Jonathan Keene's unpublished novel in his passenger seat, he knew he wouldn't be home for long.

He paused as he got out of the car, noticing the front door was slightly ajar. Cliff's Jeep Wrangler was parked under the canopy, so he shook his head and mumbled, "Fucking idiot," under his breath.

"Cliff," he shouted as he came in, "you left the goddamn front door unlatched. There's a killer on the loose!"

Music was blaring upstairs and he knew that his son was locked in his room headbanging to some garbage, unable to hear him. He tossed his briefcase down on the entryway bench and looked down at the wrinkled page in his other hand. He hadn't bothered to read this one, since the last three pages he found just retold the same nightmares that Benjamin experienced for the past twenty-one years; he had no desire to subject himself to more.

He walked back toward his study to add this page to the others, but he stopped when he noticed—felt in his guts rather than saw—something was off.

The door to his study was partially open. The only people that went into that room were himself and the maid, and Candice knew to shut the doors securely after she cleaned in there.

No one went into his study.

Throwing the doors open, he strode quickly toward his desk which had clearly been molested by an outside party; papers were scattered, his favorite fountain pen was knocked out of its base, and his desk chair was certainly not pushed in like it belonged.

And the desk drawer that contained Jonathan Keene's writing was open and empty.

Benjamin wasn't much of an athlete these days—he was bad about getting to the gym and he hadn't had a proper jog in almost six months—but he raced up the stairs to Cliff's room like he was in his twenties.

He burst into his son's room to find him lying on his bed playing that stupid Nintendo. "Were you in my study?!"

Cliff rolled over and looked at him, clearly confused. "No, wasn't Mr. Vandrel in there waiting for you?"

Oh shit, Benjamin thought. "When was he here? How long since he left?!"

"I didn't know he left. He just showed up like, I dunno, fifteen minutes ago..."

Benjamin raced back down to his study and grabbed two heavy objects from a hidden compartment in his file drawer. Cliff was on the landing when Benjamin came hustling back to the foyer.

"What's going on, Dad?"

Benjamin just put the .38 revolver in his son's hand, wrapping the teenager's fingers around its oiled grip.

"If he comes back here, you shoot him in the fucking head, son."

Tucking the other pistol (a semi-automatic .22) into his own pocket, Benjamin ran out to his car. He couldn't hear his son over the screams of Caroline Kraft in his head as she was strangled by those shadowy inhuman hands.

CHAPTER 17
CONCLUSIONS

P atrick read the page for the third time, making sure it wasn't something he had somehow written himself. The details were too exact. It got nearly everything right.

Except for that word.

He hadn't *raped* Caroline. She had come to him willingly, knowing exactly what it had meant. Patrick knew she wasn't a virgin, and if even half of what he had heard about the Kraft women was true...

Regardless, he wadded up the paper again for the fourth time since finding it in the driver's seat of his cruiser. After his encounter with Chief Burke, he was too worked up to even remember if he had locked his door, so anyone could have planted it.

But he only knew of one person who could have known the details written on that page—one living person at least—who wasn't the sheriff of Ransom Creek.

Benjamin Windsor's Mercedes had to have been doing at least forty as it peeled around the corner of Amberly Drive. Patrick shifted his cruiser out of park and followed.

Now Patrick was fully convinced: Benjamin Windsor wanted him to know just how much power he had over him. To what end? Patrick couldn't even begin to guess. All he knew was that one of them would die today, and as he reflected on the memory detailed in that crumpled paper in the passenger seat, he really couldn't care which of them sur-vived—hopefully neither of them.

Benjamin was speeding toward the north side of town, which meant he could be headed toward Marcus Vandrel's estate in Meadow Hills. Patrick knew he had to intervene before he got there, so he flipped on the sirens, wondering for the first time if Marcus and Benjamin were working together, taking out the Remains one by one.

Even just that thought convinced Patrick they were the ones that killed Jonathan and Debbie.

Surprisingly, Benjamin slowed down and put on his turn light, pulling the Mercedes to the shoulder of Forest Pine Avenue.

Patrick was relieved to see no traffic coming from either direction, which made it the perfect time to settle this. He loosened the latch on his gun's holster as he exited the cruiser.

Normally he would call the plates in, but Benjamin Windsor wasn't actually here—he was having an accident somewhere else and his body would likely never be recovered.

The walk toward Benjamin's open window had a strange calming effect on Patrick. He felt entirely in control of the situation; the world within the boundaries of Ransom Creek was exactly as it should be.

"Pat?! What the hell are you doing, man? We need to get to Marcus now!"

"You need to turn the car off, Ben."

As Patrick squared up to the window, Benjamin gave him a confused scowl. "What is this? Why's your goddamn hand on your gun?"

Patrick's face remained stone. "I found the note you left me. How'd you know she got pregnant?"

Even though Benjamin had a terrible poker face, he must have been practicing, because Patrick almost believed the confused look he gave him. "Pregnant? What—Pat, seriously, what the fuck? We don't have time for this, I think Marcus knows about the ashes."

"Because you told him, right?" He drew his gun now, slowly, to show Benjamin exactly who was in control of things—*Not you, Ben,* he thought. *You were never in control.*

"Because he was just at my house and he took them from my drawer!"

Patrick pulled the hammer back as he aimed the gun at his former co-conspirator. That was when the indignation melted from Benjamin Windsor's face. He was no longer the high and mighty city planner; he was the whiny seventeen-year-old twerp that Patrick had to convince to sabotage the ceremony that would have given Adratheon a human vessel.

"Alright, Pat, let's take a breath here. Talk to me—what's going on? Who's pregnant?"

"Did you tell Jon?" The tiniest hint of doubt crept into Patrick's mind as he contemplated pulling the trigger. "There's no other way he would have known—it could only have been you, Ben. I'm almost sorry to have to do this, but I'm running out of options. If this gets out, we're all dead anyway."

Benjamin's eyes darted downward slightly, and even before his hand moved, Patrick knew he was going for a gun, so he fired.

His aim was perfect and the shot blew a chunk out of Benjamin's shoulder. The man screamed and gave up any attempt to draw a weapon.

"Motherfucker!" His voice echoed emptily through the trees that surrounded them. They'd have a few minutes before anyone responded to the gunshot out here. "I didn't say anything, goddammit! I'm trying to tell you, it's Marcus! Someone's been sending me pages of Jonathan's book—I think he was blackmailing Vandrel!"

Whether or not Benjamin was telling the truth, the bullet had already left the chamber, and Patrick knew he couldn't let him walk. However, he lowered the gun for a moment and stepped toward the car.

"That doesn't explain how Jonathan knew we used Walter's ashes to kill Caroline. You slipped up, Ben. And now I have to clean it up. I just need you to tell me: Does Roger know?"

"Pat!" Ben was weeping now like a scared little boy. "I seriously don't know what the hell you're talking about! Someone's been leaving pages of Jonathan's book for me to find—talking about how Jon and Deb also took some of the ashes...it wasn't just us! They also didn't trust Marcus. They also didn't believe any of it would work." He grimaced against the pain. "They didn't know what we knew—how to use it against Marcus."

Patrick's gaze became distant as the logic slowly sunk in. Maybe Benjamin wasn't bullshitting him...maybe—

But before any other revelations could bloom, Benjamin made a clumsy grab for his pocket and Patrick stepped back, drew his gun again, and obliterated Benjamin Windsor's skull with a point-blank shot.

The sheriff of Ransom Creek calmly holstered his sidearm, glancing in either direction of the empty road. When his gaze settled back on Benjamin's lifeless body, Patrick saw Caroline Kraft in its place, the girl's vacant eyes forever skyward.

In those dark, phantom orbs, Patrick Larson felt a comforting sense of accomplishment.

But his work wasn't done yet.

Marcus found Roger drinking at the lodge's bar. His tie was loosened and his shirt sleeves were rolled up, as if he had been on his fourth or fifth whiskey.

The lobby was empty except for a bellboy leaning against the concierge desk and the receptionist, Claire, who gave Marcus a hesitant wave.

Ignoring her, Marcus joined Roger in the low-lit bar.

"I'll take one of whatever he's having," Marcus told the young bartender.

Roger held up a finger. "Luke, run back to the reserves and grab that bottle of Macallan for us. And tell Morris to bring out some wings or something."

Luke nodded and headed back toward the kitchen.

"Have you gotten any?" Marcus asked when they were alone.

Roger just sipped his drink with closed eyes. When he lowered his glass, he cast Marcus a weary gaze. "Did you kill them, Marcus?"

Snorting in disbelief, Marcus looked over his shoulder to make sure no one heard. "Why would I kill them?" he whispered. "I needed them, Roger. I needed all of you."

"For what?" Roger's words were slurred. "You haven't needed Jonathan since he left, and the last time the Remains met, you said you still didn't know why it hadn't worked."

"I lied," Marcus hissed through his teeth. "I know why it didn't work, and I was going to fix it. I just needed the girl to inherit the Kraft estate—that's the only way I could have replaced Walter's ashes with something more potent. I needed the heir! And it was all going as planned until Jonathan showed up!"

"Which is why you killed him, right? Because you couldn't pay him off now that you're broke."

That took Marcus aback. There was no way that Roger would have known about his family's debts from decades of chasing cult secrets all over the world. Not unless he was working with the Cranes or dealing with Rothen behind his back.

Marcus pulled the pages out of his jacket pocket, which were wrapped around the small box that contained the missing ashes of Walter Kraft. "So this was you? Leaving these little love letters from Jonathan's book at my house? And in my car? In my mail?"

Roger looked at the items, an expression of genuine confusion on his face. "I found some too... What's in the box?"

Marcus held his gaze. Of all the members of their order, Roger was always the easiest for him to read; he was a simple man that played by the rules. Marcus looked at the final dregs of whiskey in the man's glass. He was mourning Deborah Collins, his lost love.

This was not the man who betrayed the Remains and sabotaged the ritual.

This was his last chance.

Marcus set the box and the pages on the bar. "Let's have a drink, Roger. We have to discuss what to do about Patrick and Benjamin."

Chapter 18
Awake

Tori didn't want to talk about it while in the room with Rachel, who had been sleeping peacefully all evening. Eddie took a walk with her to get a coffee; neither of them planned on sleeping that night.

"When I told you before," she began, once they each had a hot beverage, "about her getting on the roof. That actually happened a couple times. Once, she was at school. I had to come get her—they said there was no way she should have been able to get up there. The janitor had to unbolt an access hatch that had been sealed for almost three years." Tori's gaze was distant as Eddie blew on his coffee. "Then she did it again at home, about a week before Marcus Vandrel came."

Eddie froze mid-sip. He waited for her to continue, but she just kept staring distantly. Finally, he asked, "Vandrel came to Rhode Island?"

She just nodded.

"Tori, what was Marcus Vandrel doing in Rhode Island?"

Blinking, she finally broke whatever spell locked her eyes on the unseen past. She looked at Eddie, and he could see how terrified she was to say whatever burdened her.

"He brought my grandfather's will, to show me the clause in the trust that would require us to move back to Ransom Creek if we wanted to inherit the estate."

Eddie's heart raced, feeling the adrenaline that came when one of his hunches panned out. However, there were so many pieces still missing; he needed her to continue.

"Of course, I didn't even want the estate," she added. "After everything that happened in this fucking town—I didn't want to bring Rachel here. But then..."

"Did he threaten you?"

Tori recoiled slightly. "Marcus? No, of course not. He was very kind. It was Rachel... While Marcus and I discussed my hesitations, I noticed Rachel—who was watching TV, just ten feet from us—catatonic again. Of course, I panicked. But when I went to her, she stood up and glared at Marcus." Tori's voice caught in her throat. "She looked like—I swear she looked just like Caroline."

Eddie put an arm around her and pulled her closer. He felt like he should tell her to stop, but he needed to know. So, he gave her a moment.

"I don't remember her enough," Tori said, still sniffing. "But I just felt like I was looking at my sister. And then she started talking to Marcus in some...it was like utter nonsense, Eddie. A language I can't even descr ibe... I still hear her sometimes at night, speaking what just sounds like pure evil."

Eddie wasn't sure what to make of any of this yet, but it sounded like Rachel might have some sort of schizophrenia or something. He made a mental note to ask her doctor about it.

"That's why we came back here," Tori said. Her voice was steadier now as she added, "Because Marcus said he could help her. He said—you're gonna think I'm crazy, Eddie—but if you would have heard her..."

"What'd he say?"

She finally took a drink of her coffee. "He said Caroline told him when they were in school that she believed my grandfather cursed her. And the only way to break that curse was for Rachel to inherit the estate."

It took everything Eddie had not to laugh.

Later that night, Eddie stirred awake, not realizing where he was. Seeing Tori curled up nearby on the double-seated bench beside him reminded Eddie that he was still at the hospital. He yawned and stretched the stiffness from his back, but it wasn't until he rubbed his eyes that he noticed Rachel was gone.

He jerked up in his seat, feeling his heart trying to climb out of his throat. His instinct was to not wake up Tori and cause her to panic, so he stepped away from her as silently as he could. Before he was able to make it toward the door, a toilet flush drew his gaze to the strip of light coming from the room's adjoining restroom. Eddie felt silly as he released an uneven breath that had been trapped in his chest.

Rachel Kraft stepped into the darkness. She looked at Eddie with an unreadable expression on her face.

"I didn't want to wake Mom up," she whispered. "How long was I gone this time?"

Eddie gave Tori a quick glance—she was still snoring softly—before telling Rachel, "About five days..." He looked at the glowing hands of his watch. "Maybe six."

When he looked up, he saw that Rachel was staring at the badge on his belt.

"Am I in trouble?"

Eddie took a careful step toward her, lowering himself slightly so he didn't have to speak down to her. "What do you remember, Rachel?" He tried to ask it calmly and quietly, but he had a million questions he wanted to get through before Tori woke up. "Do you remember anything from earlier today?"

Rachel didn't hesitate. "I thought I went to the party today, but you said I've been gone almost six days... It was Friday. Mom was working late and I didn't want to stay in the trailer all night. I saw Elijah leaving his place while I was sitting on the porch, and he invited me to come along."

Once again, Eddie resisted the urge to take out his notebook. If he stopped her to ask Elijah's last name, she might freeze up again or Tori might wake up. He had to lead her through the events, not the details. "You went with him to the party?"

Rachel shook her head. "I was scared, after what happened at lunch that day. I knew Valerie would be there."

Eddie wasn't sure what that meant, but he just nodded for her to continue.

"About an hour later, I went into the ravine. But I don't remember why. Just walked for a while until I heard..."

Eddie followed Rachel's gaze toward her sleeping mom. When he turned back to Rachel, her eyes had narrowed on him. "Did she tell you about the curse?"

He nodded.

"I heard his voice in the ravine. He told me to find his remains."

"Rachel?!"

Tori's voice startled Eddie and he nearly fell backward. She rushed over to embrace her daughter.

"Whose voice?" Eddie asked Rachel. He tried to ignore Tori's glare as he held the girl's gaze. "Whose remains?"

Rachel's lips moved but produced no sound. But somehow, Eddie heard her.

This time, the talk of curses wasn't even remotely funny.

CHAPTER 19
THE ALUMNI

Donald sorted through Anne's files, hoping that recent events and insights might give him a new perspective on things. He looked at the clock when the phone rang, wondering who in the hell needed to talk to him at 2:36 in the morning.

"Hello?"

"Don, I was just going to leave a voicemail."

"Eddie?"

"Listen, we need to talk. Now."

"Let's just meet at the station in a few hours—not like I'll be getting any sleep." He looked at the contents of Anne's investigation spread across his kitchen table.

"This can't wait, man. Rachel's awake."

"Well, shit! Jesus, man, I'll come there."

Eddie paused. "We can't grill her now. She's with her mom and a nurse. Besides, we have some other shit to deal with."

Donald rubbed his eyes. "Guess I'll put some coffee on then."

Fourteen minutes later, Eddie and Donald both stood hunched over the extent of Anne Warren's investigation.

"Alright," Donald began, holding a hand over the chaotic stacks of notes, reports, and photos, "if somehow Rachel Kraft believes she is possessed by the ghost of her aunt...which I don't even know how to process..."

Eddie looked up, and something other than exhaustion seemed to age the man's face under the dim glow of the kitchen's overhead light. But he just shook his head and told Donald, "Doesn't matter, right? We just follow the facts. And the fact is, however Rachel might know what really happened to her aunt is irrelevant—we just need to find the connection here." Eddie pointed to a newspaper clipping about the Vandrel Group acquiring twenty acres of land south of Ransom Creek for commercial property development.

Donald shook his head. "I don't like Marcus for this. I get the connections, but you're looking at the most connected guy in North Carolina." Donald pushed that article aside and revealed a Valley High yearbook photo of Marcus with Benjamin Windsor lifting up a third teenager. "I'm more inclined to suspect Windsor having the answers we need. His dad ran the paper when Keene wrote that fluff piece about Caroline's death... There's gotta be something there."

"Alright, well, clearly he's tighter with Marcus than he's letting on," Eddie added. "And what about our other victim? Collins. She's in real estate too, right?" He tapped Vandrel's photo again. "Just because the guy is too connected doesn't mean he's excluded. What about Dupree at the lodge?"

Donald pulled out a piece of notebook paper that had several sticky notes on it. "Anne told me she had a strange interview with Roger about ten years after the Caroline Kraft incident. He filed a complaint with the parks department when they presented plans to develop a hiking trail or something too close to his planned lodge expansion." Donald showed Eddie. "Our city planner obviously sided with Dupree, even though he still hasn't broken ground on his new lodge. In fact..."

Donald shuffled through the files to produce another piece of paper. "Just two years ago, Anne found this zoning permit that shows the Rothen Corporation was building a research center there."

Eddie took the paper, but Donald could tell the man really had no idea what he was looking at. "These high rollers—Vandrel, Collins, Keene, Dupree, Windsor—seems like they were all pretty close, and yet none of them seem to know anything about Keene's murder."

"I doubt they'd know much about the Collins murder either," Donald offered, looking at his watch. "Jesus, Eddie. The sun will be up soon. Let's pack this up and take it to the station, maybe grab a bite and a shitload of coffee on the way."

"Is that the sheriff?"

Donald focused his gaze on Eddie, who was pointing to the yearbook image of Marcus and Benjamin hoisting up a third person; Patrick Larson was almost unrecognizable with such a strange look on his face.

He actually looked happy.

Roger was at the sheriff's office first thing in the morning. Darlene let him into Pat's office after Roger insisted he had some important information regarding the Jonathan Keene murder case.

Patrick arrived as several of the night-shift deputies convened in the breakroom. He barely acknowledged Roger as he entered the office and closed the door.

"You look like shit," Roger said in greeting. And he did. Patrick Larson aged better than most of them, staying in peak physical condition. But he walked with slumped shoulders today, and Roger would bet money that the man didn't sleep last night.

Not like Roger had either though.

"Long night. What do you need, Roger?"

Taking a dramatic breath, Roger considered where to even begin. "I think Marcus killed Jon. Maybe Deb too."

Patrick regarded him calmly from behind his desk. "Got some proof?"

"Since when do you need proof?!" Roger surprised himself with that retort, having always avoided any confrontations with the alpha of their little crew. However, Pat didn't seem to react, which was almost even more unsettling. Roger leaned forward in his chair. "Did you know Marcus was losing his company? The Cranes are pushing him out. He's fucking broke, which is why he's been stalling on the northern lodge."

"He's broke, so he killed Jonathan Keene? Doesn't make any sense."

"Keene was fucking blackmailing him, Pat. He told me himself when he came to the lodge...probably just to stage some kind of alibi or something."

Roger was quite stunned to see how none of this seemed to affect the sheriff. Had he possibly gotten this all wrong? Did Patrick already know who the murderer was, and now Roger was painting a target on his own back with the other members?

No, he thought. This felt too right.

"So you're saying Marcus is the one who's been planting all these pages from Jonathan's book?"

Roger nodded, relieved to at least see that Patrick was following. "He came to the lodge last night. He tried to make me think that you and Ben were the ones who killed Jon and Deb. And I played along, because, who knows... He might have killed me!"

Patrick drummed his fingers on the desk, looking out the windows of his office. "He might have. Which means he might kill Ben—maybe already has." Patrick gave him a strange look then. "We need to keep him thinking he has the upper hand. Where is he today?"

"We actually have a meeting in an hour," Roger admitted. "I absolutely need to close that deal with Rothen before anything else happens." He did not tell Patrick about the Rothen soldiers who would be at the meeting, ensuring Roger stayed alive; as long as he proved his worth to the company, that is.

"Good," said. "Take care of that, and then keep him there. I'll meet you there and take care of him."

Roger felt uneasy. "Are you sure, Pat? I mean...what are you gonna do? Arrest him?"

Patrick stood up and adjusted his belt. "Just gonna ask him a few questions. Steer clear of the cops too. I have to take care of those detectives next."

"Why the hell are we going back to the school?"

Donald tried to straighten his tie as he drove. "We can have whatever suspicions we want, Eddie. But we're not taking anything to the chief until we have something extremely fucking solid."

"I get that, buddy, trust me. I'm not looking forward to stepping in the sheriff's shit unless we're a hundred percent sure we got a lock on him. But we still have the Collins autopsy and following up with Dupree. What are we looking for at the school?"

Donald explained the situation with Valerie Collins, and it brought back to mind the thing Rachel had mentioned about being scared of going to the party. His mind was racing and he felt like he was losing track of which case they were actually trying to solve.

As they pulled into the school, the buses were just unloading students. Donald parked along the sidewalk near the main entrance and they made their way in to see Principal Vickers.

"Ah, yes," the man said, when asked about the incident between Valerie Collins and Rachel Kraft. "I meant to call you about that. It slipped my mind when you were here last."

Eddie glanced pointedly at Donald before looking back at Barry. "Seems like a pretty important thing to forget, given Rachel was missing at the time."

Vickers didn't seem nervous as he said, "Yes, I feel terrible that I may have hindered your investigation due to my forgetfulness—my sister keeps saying I should just retire before I forget where I work." He gave an unenthusiastic laugh. "However, I understand you've found Rachel, yes?"

"How did you hear that?" Donald asked.

"Oh, her mother called and left a message this morning, saying she would be absent. Is she alright?"

Eddie nodded. "She'll be alright. Did you hear she was found at the scene of a murder?"

The man gasped, looking at Donald and then back to Eddie. "Dear god..."

Donald explained that the reason they wanted to know more about the incident on Friday was because of who the victim of the murder was.

"I can't believe it," Barry said, his eyes drifting toward his framed photos on the wall. His gaze suddenly jerked back to Eddie. "You can't think that Rachel Kraft could have done something like that?"

"We were hoping you might be able to tell us," Eddie said. He did his best to rattle the principal with his gaze, but the man just seemed genuinely upset. "Besides the incident Friday, can you tell us about any other run-ins Rachel may have had with the Collins girl?"

Barry inhaled a shrug and shook his head. "Honestly, being the new girl, Rachel mostly kept to herself. Not that I'm keeping up with all the different cliques in school, but the few times I saw her in the halls, she was either walking alone or talking with Elijah Weathers—you know, Betsy," he said to Donald. "I believe she had that misunderstanding with Roger Dupree...some legal thing. Elijah lives in Bright Hollow, so you might want to speak with him in regards to Rachel's social life."

"We will," Donald said, shifting in his seat as he jotted something in his notebook. "Speaking of Roger Dupree, I was hoping you might be able to tell us a little about your time as vice principal."

Eddie noticed something then: the faintest twitch at the corner of Barry's mouth. But he just inclined his head and told Donald, "I'd be happy to...as much as I can remember at least." His laugh was more enthusiastic, but Eddie suspected it was forced.

Donald motioned to the wall of framed photos. "We noticed you didn't have the senior class photo for the class of 1974. Given the circumstances, I get it. But we'd like to know what you remember about some of the students."

"Roger Dupree?" Barry asked.

"Among others," Donald replied. "My partner and I spoke with Benjamin Windsor, who mentioned he ran in the same circles as Dupree, Collins, Keene, and Vandrel."

"And Larson," Barry added. "They had quite a reputation, given who their parents were." Eddie noticed that the old man's eyes narrowed as he looked toward his wall of photos. "Those kids ruined a sweet, young girl..."

Eddie shared a sidelong glance with Donald before urging the principal on. "You mean Caroline Kraft?"

The name drew Barry's eyes back to him. "Yes. Sorry, I know it's a bit uncouth to discuss such...complicated events in Ransom Creek's past. But I do believe young Marcus Vandrel had quite the obsession with the Kraft family."

"What makes you say that?" Donald asked.

"Well, he was stalking the poor girl," Barry snapped, emotion finally finding its way into his normally steady voice. "I'm sure I can find records of all the complaints we had from Jeremiah and Monica Kraft, urging me to discipline Arthur Vandrel's boy. That family feud goes back decades though, so we..." Barry spun slightly in his chair, as if ashamed. "I regret that I did not take the complaints as seriously as I should have. I know there was an investigation into Caroline's death, and it was ruled an accident. But you'll excuse me if I do not fully believe that Marcus Vandrel was innocent that night... Whatever truly happened, I don't think Caroline would have been there if it wasn't for him."

"And what about the sheriff?"

Eddie's question drew both men's gaze, but it was Donald's smoldering eyes that Eddie could almost feel.

"What about him?" Barry asked.

Eddie leaned forward, elbows on his knees. "Well, he was friends with Marcus, right? And his father was a sheriff's deputy at the time of the investigation..."

Donald closed his notebook and began to get out of his chair.

"Well, I, uh," Barry stammered. "If you're implying there was any improper—"

"Thank you for your time, Principal Vickers," Donald said as he buttoned his jacket. "You've been very helpful."

Eddie had no choice but to follow his partner out. Donald didn't say anything to him, and walked swiftly toward the exit.

Once they got outside, Donald spun on Eddie and pushed him up against the school's brick wall. "From now on you just shut up and let me handle these interviews. You're going to fuck this investigation up!"

Eddie slapped the man's hand off him. "This investigation is already fucked, Don! You think we're gonna find any answers by toeing your precious line? In case you missed it back there, it sounds like our prime suspects are pretty much running your fucking town! The rules are out the window now—the only way to find out what really happened with Rachel and her aunt is by doing it our own way."

Donald glared at him, but Eddie could tell he was having trouble finding a hole in the logic.

"Get in the car," he finally said. "It's time we brought in Marcus Vandrel."

Patrick watched the encounter from around the corner of the school. He wasn't entirely sure what the detectives were bickering about, but he doubted it was them celebrating finding a break in the case.

He allowed himself a small smile, feeling like maybe he had a little bit of time before they posed a serious threat.

Once Avery's car pulled away, he went in to close the last loop before taking care of Marcus Vandrel.

Valley High felt particularly strange to Patrick as he passed through the entrance. He remembered all the times he had passed through those doors as a teenager, eager to bask in the peak years of his life—back when all he had to worry about was playing football and working his way through the cheerleading squad.

Before going to the principal's office, Patrick walked over to the Valley High Wall of Fame, where various graduates were featured for their various accomplishments. Jonathan Keene and Deborah Collins were side-by-side, their year of death not yet added. Neither was Benjamin Windsor's. Patrick's gaze fell on Roger Dupree and he wondered if by the end of the day it would only be his own picture not destined to have a *1995* after the birth year.

Looking up at Marcus Vandrel at the top of the alumni next to his father, Arthur Vandrel, Patrick knew that particular family line would indeed end before the sun went down.

He went to see Principal Vickers just as the school bell rang.

"Sheriff," Barry said, sounding every bit his age as Patrick slipped into his office and closed the door. He made a point not to knock. "What can I do for you?"

"You can stand up and put your hands behind your back, Principal Vickers."

Barry's eyes widened. "I didn't say anything to them, Patrick. They were asking about Rachel Kraft, not... Why don't you sit down so we can talk?"

Patrick gave him the most condescending smile he could muster as he rested his hands on the back of a chair facing the principal's desk. "I was certain Jon's book was mostly just a way to extort Marcus, but some of the pages I got were just a little too personal... It was almost like he had co-written that thing, or at least helped Jonathan with the details."

Barry swallowed. A bead of sweat trailed down the side of his wrinkled brow.

Patrick knew the look of the guilty. "Jon Keene was always a quirky guy, but he rarely made things personal; if anything, he's what I might call a nihilist. However, whoever wrote about Caroline refusing the abortion that I was going to fucking pay for... Well, those are the kind of details that weren't entirely necessary to take down Marcus Vandrel."

Sudden rage washed over Barry Vickers' face and Patrick knew his hunch had paid off. He couldn't hold back the laugh.

"You fucked her without a rubber?! You did, didn't you! Jesus, Barry! I gotta hand it to you, that's ballsy. I mean, I get the power trip—I'd probably be tapping some of Jared's girlfriends if I had your access. But bare-backing it?"

"I loved her," Barry said, his voice eerily calm. "And you raped her, you bastard."

"You loved her a little too much, old man. Look, I did you a favor—so you're welcome. Caroline was a psycho and not even that good of a lay. We had our fun and I got rid of the evidence." He straightened now, resting his hands on his belt, making sure the old man saw his gun. "But you're going to have to play ball with me if you want to retire with dignity. Now turn around and put your goddamn hands behind your back so I can cuff you."

Barry seethed for another moment, but then obeyed.

"Good man," Patrick said when the other man's back was to him. But instead of reaching for his cuffs, he slowly and silently drew his gun.

CHAPTER 20
UNDER CONSTRUCTION

The Vandrel Group's main office was on the northside of downtown, and while Donald didn't actually expect to find him there, it was as good a place as any to start their search.

"I'll do the talking," Donald reminded Eddie as they walked toward the office doors, and the silence that followed told him his partner was still sour with him. That was fine. From his limited experience, a sulky Eddie Rane was more predictable than a jolly Eddie Rane.

"Hello," Donald told the receptionist. "We were hoping to schedule an appointment with Mr. Vandrel."

The woman behind the desk looked like she just got out of college, and she seemed eager to help the police—whether it was out of respect or fear, Donald didn't care.

"Certainly," she said as she used her computer's mouse to check the big man's calendar. "It looks like Marcus will be out most of the day at a development meeting for Lot 54. Would you like me to leave a message for him?"

"Lot 54?" Donald asked. "Isn't that the site of the new Brookridge Lodge?"

The woman gave him a confused look. "I'm afraid I'm not sure about that, Officer. I believe Marcus is meeting with a representative from the Rothen Corporation in regards to the new satellite office being built on the lot."

Donald thanked her and led Eddie back out.

"That lot's been sitting vacant for almost three years, Eddie. The planning commission has been dragging their feet on several offers, but Roger Dupree has attended the meetings each month to present a pretty flimsy proposal for a new lodge."

Eddie raised his shoulders. "So what?"

Donald looked northward, where his view was blocked by the rising tree line. "I'm just wondering why there's suddenly movement at the lot when we've had two back-to-back murders..."

"We should find out," Eddie said, walking toward the car.

"What good is this going to do?" Marcus asked Roger, motioning to the armed soldier guarding the lab entrance. "Even if I sign off on this, I'm going to have to get approval from the board."

Roger waved his hands to wash that line of questioning away. "We'll worry about that once we get Benjamin the agreement. As you can see, Rothen's almost done with the first phase of their expansion. The lab's gonna go under the lodge, so we're at the perfect crossroads here to greenlight my part of the project."

Marcus eyed Roger warily, wondering if the man was hiding something. The fact that he was so insistent on pushing this forward without Patrick present was encouraging, but he couldn't shake the feeling that the man was rushing him.

And then there were the armed mercenaries. The Rothen Corps was one thing; he had become accustomed to the corporation's private military. However, these men didn't wear the black fatigues that marked Rothen's soldiers; they were dressed in mismatched urban camo and army surplus attire.

"We can go over the specifics later," Roger insisted. "But it's like you said, we need to move forward as if Benjamin and Patrick were not necessary. If anything...unexpected were to present itself, we need to have our next steps in place. And I think we can both agree that a partnership with Rothen is exactly the type of next step that this town needs."

Unexpected, Marcus thought. A strange paranoia gripped him as he eyed Roger, who was holding a pen out for Marcus to take so he could sign the agreement. Suddenly he was wondering why the hell he agreed to meet out here with everything going on. Perhaps he had been so relieved that Roger was on his side and not Patrick's or Benjamin's that he would have agreed to anything, or maybe it was just because he was curious to see what kind of progress Rothen had made without his knowledge.

In all honesty, Marcus most likely allowed the situation to play out because he didn't want to even discuss the Patrick situation anywhere near the vicinity of the sheriff's office. Even though they were still within the town limits, the lot was at least the most remote option for them to conspire.

He looked over again at the lone soldier watching them; he blocked the only way out of the construction trailer.

"Marcus?"

Looking back at Roger, he regarded the pen being extended to him. It was a Brookridge Lodge pen, but the logo was almost unreadable as the implement shook in Roger's nervous fingers.

The desire to call the man out crossed Marcus' thoughts, but he had enough of his wits to know at that moment that he had no command over the other individual in the trailer with them.

Roger had that advantage.

Marcus took the pen and bent over the nearby desk to at least make a show of signing the agreement. "Are we going to be able to notarize this before Benjamin or Patrick catch wind?"

"I'll head straight to the bank," Roger assured him. "Let's just get this signed so we can get back to more pressing matters."

Just as Marcus put the pen to the paper, wondering how long after the man filed this with the city that the truth of Marcus' financial situation would become known, the Rothen soldier's radio crackled.

"Who called the cops?"

The soldier moved toward the window and peered through the blinds. Marcus knew he'd have no better opportunity and made his move before his mind could question anything.

With everything he had, Marcus shoved Roger into the soldier and bolted for the door.

"Hey!" The soldier let out a pained grunt while Roger shouted a command that both angered and chilled Marcus.

"Shoot him! Shoot him, he's a murderer!"

Donald drew his gun when they heard the shouts from somewhere beyond the construction fences. The makeshift barriers screened his and

Eddie's view into the lot, which looked much more developed than any public records had shown.

"Multiple vehicles," Eddie said from behind, motioning to a clearing in the distance. Donald saw several spots of sunlight reflecting through the trees.

"We should go call for backup," Donald thought aloud. But Eddie was already moving past him along the fencing.

"You want the sheriff taking over?" he called over his shoulder. "Move!"

Donald didn't have time to argue as more shouts followed the sound of a door slamming shut. Through a gap in the fencing, he saw the gun before he saw the man who carried it. "Eddie, down!" Raising his sidearm, he fired into the tree where the submachine gun was emerging.

Eddie fired too, but neither of them prevented the assailant from unleashing a burst that shredded a section of fencing. Donald heard more gunfire on the other side of the fence, but he focused on the threat he could see, pumping more rounds where the gunman's torso should be.

"He's down!" Eddie was on a knee now, trying to peer through the holes in the fence. Crouching low, Donald moved toward him. "Another gunman in that trailer," Eddie said.

Before Donald could get a look, more bullets cracked around them and the detectives had to push toward the cement mixer near the main gates.

"What the fuck did we walk into?!" Eddie asked when they were in cover.

"Cover that side," Donald said, pointing to the opposite end of the vehicle. "Sounds like there's at least two of them, and I saw a third making a break for the cars. My guess is that's Vandrel."

Eddie was already firing by the time Donald confirmed his suspicion. "Marcus! Freeze!"

The fleeing figure hazarded a glance over his shoulder, his panic replaced by a peculiar look of surprise—as if he had expected someone other than the police. Maybe he hoped the sheriff was going to come rescue him from whatever shitshow they just walked into. But more gunfire made Donald duck back behind cover, losing sight of Marcus, who kept running into the woods.

"Go after him!" Eddie yelled between shots. "I'll cover you—hurry, before I have to reload!"

Donald fired twice before daring to leave cover, but fortunately it seemed like the gunmen had to reload as well. He sprinted down the trail after Marcus, still hearing the man's footsteps—it sounded like he was going down into the ravine on foot.

Where the hell are you running? Donald thought, but he immediately paid the price for letting his mind drift; he lost focus on his footing and tumbled headfirst into the ravine.

Eddie heard shouted commands between the gunmen and knew he was about to be surrounded. He jammed a fresh magazine in and crept along the cement mixer to where Donald had been near the vehicle's cabin. He doubted he'd be lucky enough for the keys to be inside, but he didn't have a ton of options.

The door was surprisingly unlocked, and he scanned the interior for options. Bullets shattered the passenger's window and Eddie cursed as he dropped to the ground. He rolled to his side to get a view under the vehicle just in time to see a prone man in mercenary garb aiming an MP5 where Eddie had just been. Instinct took over: he aimed and fired, putting a single round in the man's head.

"Taylor's down!" someone shouted. "Fall back!"

"There's only one of them!" a panicked voice replied, and Eddie could tell it was not one of the gunmen. *Is that you, Dupree?*

Eddie rolled to his knees, hoping to take advantage of the temporary reprieve.

"I said fall back, goddammit! The target's on the move!"

"Drop your weapons while you can!" Eddie shouted. "Backup is on the way! You got enough firepower in there to take on the whole police department?!"

He hadn't expected the bluff to work, but the gunfire had ceased and he heard the crackle of radio chatter, as if they were discussing alternative plans. Eddie risked a glance over the mixer's hood and saw that the shooters had indeed dispersed—the construction site was devoid of movement. The only place anyone could be hiding from Eddie was in the trailer.

"Don!" Eddie kept his eyes forward as he waited for a response, but when none came, he cautiously moved around the cement mixer with his gun moving between the trailer and each piece of intervening terrain.

Even though Eddie's heart still pushed heavy amounts of adrenaline through his body, he managed to steady his breathing now that the firing had stopped. It gave him a chance to take in the surroundings, and he was shocked to see the landscape beyond the trailer gave way to a sectioned-off basement, which was where Eddie suspected the gunmen fled to.

A rustling behind him caused Eddie to drop to one knee and turn to fire at whoever tried to ambush him. Fortunately, he was slow on the trigger this time.

"Hey! It's me!" Donald's suit was uncharacteristically disheveled, with streaks of mud across his white shirt and one of his jacket's lapels torn. He had a rip in one knee and Eddie saw blood.

"Where's Marcus?"

Donald shook his head. "Fucking got away. Fell down an incline and twisted my goddamn ankle." He limped forward with his gun raised toward the construction site. "What's the situation?"

"One down. The others ran. Guessing somewhere in that basement that's getting dug out."

Donald lowered his gun slightly as he dragged his leg and locked step with Eddie. "What the hell are they building here? None of this was here last time I came through. I heard Roger was trying to get a new lodge off the ground, but I would have heard if they broke ground."

"Ground has certainly been broken," Eddie said, quickening his step. "Come on, their vehicles are back that way, so we might be able to corner them."

Donald grabbed his shoulder. "Are you fucking nuts? Corner them?! We don't even know what we're walking into down there." He nodded back toward their car. "We need to call this in, now."

"How's that gonna play out?" Eddie scowled at him. "We give the sheriff a heads up so he has time to cover this up?" He pointed toward the hollowed-out earth. "We get just one of those assholes alive, or find Dupree down there pissing his pants, and we lay this out publicly—whatever it is."

A crackled voice interrupted whatever Donald's reply might have been.

"Crop Dusters, check in."

Avery and Rane both turned to the dead soldier, whose radio spoke again. "We have Babbling Brook. Northside, in the tunnels. No reception. Brook says get clear and call the sheriff—kill the cops."

A different voice. "Crop Duster, copy. Taylor's down. Switch channels. Over."

"Former military," Eddie said. He turned to Donald. "Can you think of any reason the owner of a lodge has hired mercenaries?"

Donald checked his pistol's chamber before nodding to Eddie. "I guess we need to go ask him, don't we?"

Chapter 21
Desperate Measures

"**I**f you're able to reach him, please tell him that Rachel is being released today so we're heading home."

"Of course," Officer Beth Hampton replied over the phone. "I'll try Detective Rane on the radio again after this call, Ms. Kraft. Give our best to your daughter—we're all so glad she's back safe."

"Thank you." Tori hung up, feeling uneasy leaving the hospital before Eddie returned. He had told Tori not to speak to any other police officers about Rachel's situation. He was particularly concerned about them saying anything about the curse. Tori felt foolish talking to him about that; she barely knew how to process her family's legacy herself, and she would never have dumped that on him if she hadn't been beside herself with grief and lack of sleep.

She used the payphone to call Trevor at work, letting him know she'd be missing her shift again, and then made her way back to Rachel's room. She was beyond ready to return home and sleep in her own bed.

A nurse intercepted Tori just as she was turning the corner to Rachel's wing.

"Oh, there you are!"

"Hi, Nurse Mayes. Thanks for loaning me change for the payphone."

The woman smiled. "Not a problem, dear. Sorry about the hospital line—they don't even allow *us* to make outside calls. Surprisingly strict phone policy here." She motioned back toward Rachel's room. "I just wanted to let you know, your father said he would be right back. He was just going to pull the car around for you both."

Tori blinked, confused. "My father?"

"Yes, the tall man—you were wearing his jacket when you came in."

Shaking her head, Tori gave the nurse an awkward laugh. "No, that's not my father. That's Rachel's principal. He just loaned me his jacket when he was at the bar one night—it was a chilly walk home. I forgot to give it back."

The nurse's face paled. "Oh... Your daughter called him Grandpa..."

Tori felt the skin on her face sag as her feigned smile soured. She rushed past the nurse, shouting, "Rachel!"

The nurse followed behind her, screaming for security.

Ruth Phillips had been dreading this day since she first started as front desk receptionist at Valley High. When she took over for Irene Miller after the woman retired on her eightieth birthday, Ruth was certain that Principal Vickers would be retiring himself. But with each passing month, she became more and more certain that the man would rather die in his office than leave his post.

Now, as she went to see why the man was late to the faculty meeting—something that would absolutely never happen unless the man had keeled over on the job—she expected, with plenty of dread, to see her very first corpse.

She knocked softly on his office door. "Principal Vickers?" No response. She knocked harder and called his name a bit louder.

Still nothing.

Ruth took a deep breath and closed her eyes as she turned the handle and pushed the door open.

She was relieved when she peeked through her squinted eyelids to see the principal's desk vacant. However, something struck her as out of place. Principal Vickers was a very tidy, organized man, and the few times she had been in his office when he wasn't there, she could still sense the old man's influence on the place.

But something wasn't right.

Whether it was the crooked chair in front of the principal's desk, or the stack of papers that were just slightly askew, Ruth could tell something had happened in the office outside of the routine.

A quick scan of the room revealed only one area that could hide the cause of the office's malignancy. As she stared at the principal's closet door, she realized for the first time how odd it was that the room even had such a fixture. None of the other offices—or even the classrooms, to Ruth's knowledge—had closets.

She didn't want to know what was in there, and it was a strange thing to her that she could even have a preference toward Principal Vickers' office closet. However, given the discomfort that seemed to consume her, she almost had no choice in the matter.

Ruth grasped the small doorknob, which was colder than she had expected, and turned. The door opened outward to reveal the lifeless body of the sheriff, who she just now realized never passed by her desk when he had arrived—she would have remembered.

Ruth wanted to scream out in horror, but something froze her in place, locking her gaze on the man's vacant eyes. Something alien prevented her from doing any of the things a rational person might do in a moment of crisis.

It was the man's neck. There was a bizarre length to it that shouldn't be possible, and black smudges colored it. In that very brief window of time when she couldn't react, Ruth imagined two large hands covered in ink wrenching at the sheriff's neck, trying to pop his head off.

Something about that image snapped her out of the trance and she was finally allowed to scream.

"Why are we skipping class just to go visit a psycho murderer in the hospital?"

Madison glared over her shoulder at Cassandra, feeling like her best friend was slowly becoming a total stranger to her. "Because she's not a murderer. I need to ask her about something." They crossed the street toward the main entrance to one of the largest buildings in Ransom Creek: Crestline Community Hospital.

"If she's still a zombie, we should go to the mall," Cassandra said. "Jared mentioned there might be a party on Friday at Cody Benson's cabin."

How could she think of going to a party after what happened to Valerie's mom? Madison got the curious impression that maybe she had contracted some affliction from the pages she had read—like she was harboring this growing dread over the recent events surrounding Rachel Kraft, but no one else could sense it.

"Oh shit!" Cassandra whispered, putting her arm out to press Madison toward the hospital's wall. "It's the principal!"

Madison peered around her friend to see Principal Vickers wearing a jacket that didn't match his suit. He had his arm around—

"That's Rachel!" Madison whispered. "What the hell is going on?"

The girls watched as their principal guided a stiff-limbed Rachel into a car parked along the curb.

"Looks like she's still a zombie," Cassie remarked. Before Madison could voice her annoyance that Cassandra was focused on Rachel's physical state as opposed to the fact that Principal Vickers seemed to be abducting her, a different car pulled up to them.

"Naughty girls," Jared Larson said from the driver's seat. Cliff Windsor sat in the passenger seat looking much less jovial than his friend. "What are you guys doing out of school?"

"I'd ask you the same thing, Jared," Cassandra teased. "But check it out: Principal Vickers is taking Rachel Kraft somewhere." She pointed toward the car just as Vickers closed Rachel's door. The man looked nervously over his shoulder back at the hospital and then shrugged out of that jacket as he made his way toward the driver's side door.

"What the hell?" Jared said. "Get in, let's follow him. Maybe he's taking her in for killing Valerie's mom."

Madison didn't love the idea of the two of them confronting Rachel without her, so she got into the back seat with Cassandra.

"What are you guys doing out of school anyway?" Cassandra asked. "You weren't going to visit the witch too, were you?"

"Hell no," Jared said, pulling back into the street to follow Vickers' car. "We were heading out to the Vandrel cabin. Cliff's dad didn't come home last night, and we think Marcus knows where he is."

That was when Cliff showed the girls the gun.

Madison's mouth went dry and it took her a moment to form the words: "What's that for, Cliff?"

He looked over his shoulder at her. "In case Marcus was the one who's been leaving me all those letters."

CHAPTER 22
BENEATH

Marcus nearly collapsed from exhaustion as he reached the winding drive up to his cabin. While he hadn't necessarily planned on visiting the property until the Krafts were back in their ancestral home—allowing him to finish the rites—he was certainly glad to see the old place.

But he had little time to admire the view: his pursuer was loudly closing in on him.

Marcus allowed himself a quick glance over his shoulder to confirm, and there indeed was a figure forcing his way through the thick overgrowth at the base of the hill.

Before Roger's goon broke free of the thicket, Marcus found surer footing on the paved drive leading up to his cabin. He didn't dare look back as he ran as fast as he could toward the side garage entrance that would give him access to his basement, where hopefully Adratheon would hear his call.

Donald took the lead down the confined stairwell, squinting against the dust-ridden atmosphere of the basement sub-level.

"This is fucking crazy," he whispered to Eddie, already regretting his impulsive decision to come after Roger, who probably knew this place well.

"What the hell are they building here?" Eddie wondered aloud, keeping his voice low. "Some kind of lab or medical center?"

"Rothen," Donald replied, motioning with his gun toward a crate at the foot of the stairs bearing the corporation's logo. "Heard rumors they were looking to expand here—didn't think the council would allow it."

Eddie nodded. "Judging from the look of this place and the fact that a band of mercenaries are occupying it, I'm going to say none of this is exactly above bar."

"Get out of here!"

Donald recognized Roger's voice, even though he had never heard the man sound so hysterical. It echoed down the hallway, which ended in a T about fifty feet from their position.

"They've taken me hostage and want to talk to the sheriff! Get him here now!"

Donald nodded over his shoulder at Eddie before cautiously walking toward the voice.

"They're dealing with us, Roger," Donald called back, hugging the left wall as he stepped over tools and building materials. "Sheriff's already on his way, so how about we get some of the formalities out of the way while we wait."

"Get back up those stairs," a different voice called out. "We'll pop this motherfucker if you come any closer."

"No you won't!" Eddie shouted back with disdain. "Babbling Brook? C'mon, guys. He's clearly your contact here—if he was expendable, you wouldn't be hiding down here. Seems like Vandrel was your target, and he got away. So let's call this a wash, yeah?"

Once again, Donald saw the gun at the end of the hall before it began pumping rounds at them. He took cover behind a barrel, waiting for the spray and pray to end. He looked across the hall to make sure Eddie didn't get caught in the line of fire.

However, all he saw was unfinished drywall with a single vent access cut into it. Donald called his partner's name into the darkness beyond the wall, wondering if Eddie had somehow dove through the hole like some freaking gymnast.

The only answer he got was more gunfire.

Eddie couldn't see a thing, but he heard plenty; the submachine gun thundered in these confines, and the echoes made it hard to determine the source, but he ran toward his best guess. Donald called after him, and he felt like a dick not responding, but it would give his position away.

After only a few stumbling lunges, he collided painfully with a wall and dropped his gun. He bit down on both lips to avoid cursing just as the gunfire died down. When Eddie dropped to his knees to feel around in the dark for his weapon, he heard the unmistakable sound of a magazine dropping to the floor.

It was now or never.

He got to his feet and pushed himself off the wall only to collide with another.

Only this time, he had much more force behind him...

Donald heard the click of the gunman's empty weapon, and for some reason his mind was only on Madison as he exploded to his feet. Wanting nothing more than to see his daughter again, he charged the corner at the end of the hall, closing the gap just as he heard a fresh magazine click into place.

He rounded the corner to see a crouched man in urban camo kneeling within reach. Time froze as Donald saw the man look up with wide eyes below a black bandana. The man's gun wasn't positioned to cut Donald in half yet, but the soldier just behind him had his weapon aimed right at Donald's head.

In that suspended moment that would be Donald Avery's final conscious experience, he thought of his daughter and how much he had left unsaid.

Time snapped back into place as the wall behind both mercenaries exploded inward, knocking both men forward, their weapons firing wildly.

Someone screamed from farther down the hall, but Donald paid it no mind as he dove on top of the nearest mercenary. He could hear the other attacker struggling with Eddie, who Donald now realized had just saved his life.

"You're both under arrest!" Donald shouted, putting his knee on the face-down man's neck, producing his cuffs from behind his back as he kept his gun aimed at the man Eddie wrestled with. "Give it up!" He couldn't get a clear shot—all he could do was make sure he collared his own captive before helping Eddie.

Just as Donald got the cuffs on the mercenary, Eddie let out a pained cry.

"Fuuuuck!"

Donald aimed down his sights to fire, but Eddie was on his knees, reaching for the hilt of a knife jammed into his side just below the belt; he was screening Donald's line of sight to the now fleeing soldier.

"Down! Rane, get down!"

But Eddie just yanked the combat knife out and turned to him. "I got him."

"Are you fucking crazy?! Rane! Wait for backup!"

But Eddie was already running with a slight limp down the hall, a bloodied knife held blade down in his fist.

There wasn't enough time to properly anoint Walter's missing ashes, so Marcus just dumped the box he had found in Benjamin's drawer with the rest of the old man's remains in the oversized cup.

The Chalice of Adratheon wasn't some object of great power. Marcus was fairly certain the thing was only fifty or sixty years old, likely custom made by one of Walter Kraft's murdered disciples. There were many rumors about how the Cult of Alternus dwindled down to just a few paranoid members, and Marcus' father was entirely convinced that Walter killed them all to prevent them from killing him.

Regardless, the silver vessel adorned with onyx—polished black stones that looked like wide, sinister eyes—served as good an urn as any. Marcus had just needed what his deceivers had stolen from him twenty years ago.

His hand shook as he lit the six black candles, each one positioned roughly six feet from the chalice in the center of the circle. It was the same setup the Remains had in the basement of the Brookridge Lodge, but the sixth candle that he lit now had never been properly burned.

And it would remain that way.

The intruder kicked in the door, causing a gust of wind to blow the flame from Marcus' lighter out just before the wick could take it.

"Put 'em up, Vandrel!" The Rothen-funded merc wore dark green fatigues with body armor and plenty of ammo strapped to his limbs. "You still have papers to sign, asshole."

Marcus was too cowardly to disobey, so he slowly raised his hands. Death had never felt so close to him as it had now. He knew what was needed of him and he was running out of ways to make himself valuable to a town that was feeling increasingly foreign to him.

"What good is my signature going to do?"

The man raised his gun and stepped closer. "You think I give a shit? I'm getting paid to deliver a signed document, and I'm not leaving without it."

Marcus wondered if there was any realistic way he could flick the lighter on, get it to the candle, and say the Alternian words that would summon Adratheon's wrath before this man filled him with lead.

As if he could read his thoughts, the man took another step forward and said, "You won't need both arms to sign, so don't try me. Now g—"

The threat was choked off by black smoke encircling his neck. Marcus gasped, feeling a familiar coldness that could only be eldritch magic. The smoke took shape, forming a massive hand with long, bone-like fingers.

It was the same black hand that choked the life from Caroline Kraft, and a twin version of that hand clamped down on the mercenary's arm. The revolting sound of bones snapping made Marcus recoil as he watched the gun fall from limp, fractured fingers. All the while the man's legs flailed as his head was pulled farther from his shoulders. The sickening popping sound reminded him of when he threw up during Caroline Kraft's murder.

As those black hands finished their work, their victim fell to the floor in a heap, revealing a black-haired girl staring at Marcus with vacant eyes.

"Caroline?!"

Eddie turned so sharply around the third corner that he slammed into the wall on the other side of the hallway. But he could see his fleeing assailant, the son of a bitch who was responsible for the knife wound that stained one side of his jeans a dark shade of red.

The merc had also stumbled, but was getting to his feet now that he realized he was cornered. He faced Eddie, drawing another knife from his boot.

"Just play dead, man." He pointed his serrated combat knife at Eddie before spinning it. "Lay down there and tell your partner that you got light-headed from blood loss. You're not taking me in—I don't want to kill anyone today, but I will."

Eddie didn't spin his knife, fearing that all the blood would make him lose his grip on it. Instead, he just raised it defensively and said, "I'm a shitty actor, man. The only way you're getting by me is if I'm actually dead."

The merc charged, knife raised for a downward slash. Eddie turned sideways to make a smaller target and cocked his arm back to stab the man when he swung wide. The merc spun away from the attack, using his momentum from the failed slash to shoulder Eddie against the wall.

"Agh!" Eddie cried, feeling the wound on his left hip scream as his body weight slammed into it. He reached his left hand back as he repositioned for the next attack. But he was too late; the man's knife dug into his other hip. Despite the pain, Eddie still managed to whip his cuffs around to latch onto the merc's wrist while he tried pulling the knife free.

Eddie felt like he was going to black out from the pain when he heard Donald approaching around the corner.

"You piece of sh—" the merc began, but Eddie used every ounce of his remaining strength to slam his forehead into the bastard's nose.

Both of them crumpled to the ground in a heap.

Marcus had to sit on the floor so he wouldn't faint. He knew now that it wasn't Caroline, but Rachel Kraft's presence was still too overwhelming for him.

"You feel that, don't you?"

She sounded like a man to Marcus, but her mouth wasn't moving. She just stared at him, the shadows deepening around her.

"Caroline's wrath has never left this place, it just slept until her blood returned to where our child was murdered."

Marcus realized then that it wasn't Rachel speaking to him—she looked unable to talk, as if she were under some sort of hypnotic trance. The light from the five burning candles intensified then, illuminating a tall figure behind Rachel.

"You?" Marcus blinked, feeling like he was going blind as visions from the past assaulted him. "How did you know?"

Principal Barry Vickers held up a stack of loosely bound papers. "Jonathan's book was very descriptive."

CHAPTER 23
THE REMAINING RITES

"**G**o get Dupree," Eddie urged in a slurred voice as Donald rolled him over.

"You're bleeding out, Rane. Here, get off the guy, he's out cold."

Eddie let out a pained grunt as he got himself into a sitting position. "He hit the bone. I'll be fine. Don't let that asshole get away."

"You sure you'll be alright?" Donald took another look and doubted Eddie could risk losing much more blood.

But he gave Donald a half-hearted grin. "Cavalry's gotta be on the way. We made quite a racket, partner. Go make sure it wasn't for nothing."

Donald took a second to ensure the handcuffed prick was definitely knocked out and then ran back down where he came, turning down a different unfinished corridor.

Eddie let himself go limp once he was alone.

"That's his car there," Cliff said. "What are the freaking odds he brought Rachel here? To Marcus Vandrel's cabin?!"

Madison didn't want to say, but she wasn't surprised at all.

Jared just shook his head. "Something's going on, man. Between Valerie's mom, your dad going missing, and my old man acting fucking crazy... Seems like we just need to handle this shit ourselves."

"Handle what?" Cassandra asked. The fear in her voice somehow emboldened Madison, as if she were offended that her friend couldn't cope with what was happening.

But she didn't even know how she was coping. After that scene in the school restroom—how she actually felt Rachel's presence while reading that cryptic note—something had allowed Madison to accept the fact that *unreality* was somehow a concept she could rationalize.

Whether or not any of this made sense to her, she knew that she wanted to see it through. After hiding so much from her father, it somehow felt like it was her responsibility to witness what was about to happen.

Jared put the car into park and turned to answer Cassandra. "We're going to see why our principal just kidnapped the girl who maybe just murdered our friend's mom."

"And why he's having some secret meeting with a guy my dad told me to kill," Cliff added. Madison could see that he still held the gun.

"So we're just going to go in there?" Cassandra's voice had gone up several octaves.

Once again, her friend's fragile nature urged Madison into action, and she was the first to open the door. "Whatever Rachel did, I don't like the idea of two creeps keeping her captive in a remote cabin. We can't just leave."

"Yeah," Cassandra pleaded, "but we can go get the cops. Jared, your dad's the freaking sheriff! And, Maddie, you're dad's a detective!"

"And Marcus probably pays them both," Cliff said, also getting out. "Like Jared said, we need to handle this ourselves. I know this guy knows where my dad is."

Madison was the first one to move toward the cabin, but her friends were right behind her.

Down below, Rachel stood as still as stone, staring at her grandfather's remains on the central pedestal, kept in that ridiculous chalice.

Marcus was entranced by the girl, as if just now truly realizing how much she looked like her dead aunt.

"What'd you do to her?" Marcus asked. He didn't have to look at the old man to realize he had the dead Rothen soldier's gun; he could hear Vickers checking the ammo.

"I didn't do anything," he replied. "I simply studied what you did to her—you and those entitled brats, with your cloaks and hoods and arcane meddling."

Marcus turned away from the girl now, looking doubtfully at Barry. "Are you trying to tell me she *is* Caroline?"

He aimed the gun at Marcus, his lined face fractured into a hundred angry creases. "Caroline is gone, thanks to you. The world will never see another like her." He turned slightly toward Rachel. "But her rage lingers in these trees, Marcus. That much you couldn't kill."

"Stop with the soliloquy, Vickers," Marcus snapped, looking back at Rachel. "What the fuck is this? What do you actually want?"

When Barry looked at him, Marcus felt old emotions rise within—not fear specifically, but a deep dread that was more terrifying because it felt so familiar and he couldn't recall what originally birthed it.

"I just want this to end, Marcus," Barry said, almost pleadingly. "I want to put her ghost to rest. When you killed our unborn child, you put this on me." He raised the gun higher. "She demands justice, and one of your disciples still awaits judgement. So we're going to go find him."

Marcus was beyond caring about Roger Dupree's life, but he did not want to do this old bastard's dirty work. He cautiously let his eyes shift from the gun to Rachel, wondering if he could somehow use her as a shield to make his escape.

But the footsteps came down the stairs before he could muster the courage to move.

Marcus watched as four more teens entered the basement, their faces familiar. Children of the Remains, with the exception of a brown-haired girl he didn't immediately recognize.

The four teens stopped when they caught sight of Rachel Kraft, but their eyes widened when they saw their principal aiming a submachine gun at Marcus.

That was when Benjamin's son put his own gun on Marcus as well. "Where's my dad?!"

"Principal Vickers?" Cassandra Collins gasped. "What are you doing here?"

"Why did you take Rachel from the hospital?" the brown-haired girl asked him before Cassandra even finished her question.

"You shouldn't be here, kids," Barry said, still staring at Marcus. "And why exactly do you have a firearm, Mr. Windsor?"

"Because my dad told me to shoot Marcus if I saw him—then he never came home!" Cliff jerked the pistol at Marcus. "Where is he?!"

"Your principal probably killed him," Marcus said, looking from Cliff to Jared. "I'm sure he killed your father too, otherwise he'd be here by now." Then he looked at Cassandra. "He already said he wanted to kill your dad."

"Enough," Barry snapped. "You think these kids are going to believe your lies, Vandrel? Look at your basement, for Christ's sake! You're some kind of crazy hypnotist posing as a warlock or something! Look what you did to this young girl!" He motioned toward the statue-like figure of Rachel Kraft with his gun, then to the dead soldier. "I only brought her here so he could undo it! But then I saw him with his latest victim here!"

Marcus laughed. "You're good, old man. Very clever."

Patrick's son stepped forward. "How about you both shut the fuck up! Just tell us where Cliff's dad is or he's going to shoot you both."

Marcus saw Benjamin's son nervously twitch at that suggestion.

"Rachel knows where he is," Barry said calmly. "We just need to get Marcus to snap her out of this trance he got her in."

"How?" Jared demanded.

Barry smiled at Marcus. "Each of you go stand by one of his magic candles."

Donald found Roger Dupree struggling to open a chain link construction fence secured by a padlock.

"You're cornered, Dupree," he told him, keeping his nearly empty gun trained on the terrified man.

"Please don't shoot!" Roger's hands shot upward. "Just take me in! Get me away from Marcus!"

"Slow down," Donald demanded. "Who are these soldiers, and how many more are out there?"

"They're with Rothen! There were four of them, but I don't know where the other two went. I swear!"

Donald had about a hundred more questions about Rothen having mercenaries in Ransom Creek, but he focused on the immediate situation. "Where's Vandrel?"

Roger looked over his shoulder, ever so slowly. "He's the murderer, Don. I know he is."

"Where is he, Roger?!"

Roger's eyes wandered, searching his panicked mind for possibilities. "His cabin..."

Donald knew the cabin he was talking about, and he suddenly felt absolutely dense for not assuming that's where he would have gone after escaping into the woods. But before Donald could follow up, there was an unearthly chill that filled the dark room.

Roger's eyes went wide, looking at something over Donald's shoulder. Not wanting to turn his back on a flight risk like Dupree, Donald stepped to the side and peered back into the hall. But the only thing he saw were shadows.

Donald turned back to Roger and gasped.

The man's face was a twisted mask of pain as a black writhing mass strangled him, trying to pull his head off. Not able to truly process what he was seeing, Donald stumbled backward, nearly dropping his gun as he reached out for something to keep his balance. Roger let out a pitiful croaking sound as his limbs flailed wildly. Donald felt powerless as he pulled up his gun, not sure where to fire to stop the horrible act.

All he could do was watch the man die...

"What the fuck?!" Jared cursed, pulling his hands away from the burning black candle as if it were a hot coal. He looked over at the principal, who still held his gun toward Marcus. "What the fuck just happened?!"

"The last rites," Marcus said, letting his own hand slowly fall from the candle. The heavy weight in his stomach might have been guilt for having sealed an old friend's fate without much hesitation. But in actuality, it was just the realization setting in that he had no escape from what Barry Vickers intended to do to him.

Because he had attempted to do it himself twenty-one years ago, and no one could talk him out of it then. He was only thwarted through betrayal.

"Wa-was that...my dad?" The Dupree girl's eyes glistened as she stared at the candle. She looked up to Marcus and then Barry. "You said we were just waking Rachel up..."

Rachel stood in the center of the encircling candles, still a motionless wraith.

"Only one more Remains," Barry said, his ominous tone adding weight to the sinister tumor growing in Marcus' bowels.

"He just made you kill your dad," Marcus said to Cassandra, not even caring if Barry shot him at this point. "He's killed each of your parents for what we did in 1974. I wasn't sure before, but now I understand. All we wanted to do was—"

"Was use an innocent girl to serve as your god's vessel," Barry finished.

"What the fuck are you guys even talking about?!" Jared demanded angrily. "Cliff, shoot one of them already." But everyone ignored him.

"Madison," Cassandra wept, "did we just see my dad die?!"

"Did you do that to my dad?!" Cliff demanded, stepping toward Marcus with his gun drawn.

But when he stepped beyond his candle's altar, both Barry and Marcus shouted for him to stop.

They were too late.

Cliff felt the air around him shift, like he just stepped out of a quiet shelter into a raging windstorm. His vision faded momentarily; one second he saw the horrified faces of Marcus Vandrel and Principal Vickers, and then nothing. Just inky darkness that seemed to swallow the flow of time.

When his vision returned, a different world surrounded Cliff Windsor, and his mind couldn't quite comprehend it. The weird ritual basement was gone, replaced by undulating mists that somehow reminded him of a spray of blood frozen in time.

A sudden shriek—like nails on a chalkboard but amplified through a loudspeaker—caused Cliff to try to reach for his ears, but his arms were pinned at his sides. The sound faded as quickly as it had come, but the vision that appeared before him then was even worse.

Rachel Kraft was still motionless, but her head was lowered and her eyes were fixed on Cliff—not her eyes, but a dragon's eyes set in her skull like two misplaced gemstones. Two black wings rose up from her back, spreading outward to screen Cliff from what little light pierced this void. The girl sprouted multiple dark appendages, and that was when Cliff began pulling the trigger.

At first, the gun didn't seem to react to him squeezing it frantically, but time eventually caught up and the gun went off twice before the huge monstrous entity inhabiting Rachel Kraft sprang to life and grabbed the teenager.

"Release me!" a demonic voice demanded while Rachel Kraft strangled the life out of Cliff Windsor.

Before his vision faded forever, Cliff saw frozen sprays of blood where his gunshots had ripped into Rachel's body. The girl's limbs slowly flew upward, as if she were being pulled up from some watery depths.

But Cliff was sinking into a much darker abyss...

CHAPTER 24
ADRATHEON'S CALL

D onald made sure Eddie stayed conscious as he started the car. "You still with me, partner?"

Eddie managed a weak laugh. "I won't be napping again, man. Had the weirdest fucking dream back there..."

After shifting into drive, Donald grabbed the radio. "Tell me all about it on the way," he replied. "Just keep those eyes open." He clicked the radio's handset. "Beth, it's Avery and Rane! We need backup at Vandrel's place up on Canary Hill."

"We have a unit en route that way," Beth replied. Donald heard a lot of activity in the background; Beth was almost shouting to be heard over it. "We had some reports of gunfire—what the hell's going on out there?"

"Just send another unit to Vandrel's place!" Donald made a tight turn out of the gravel parking lot. "Marcus Vandrel is wanted for questioning for the murder of Jonathan Keene, Deborah Collins, and..." he glanced at Eddie before adding, "and Roger Dupree."

"Ah, shit," Eddie mumbled under his breath. Without Dupree, everything now rested on getting Marcus in alive.

"Send paramedics too," Donald commanded. "Rane's been stabbed and he's lost a lot of blood."

"I'm fine..." Eddie began, still groaning.

"On it," Beth interrupted, but before Donald could set the radio down, she added, "Tori Kraft's reported Rachel missing again. And,

Don, there's been an incident at the school. Sheriff Larson is dead—his body was found in the principal's office."

Donald yanked the wheel as he took another corner sharply to get onto the winding road leading up Canary Hill.

"Fucking Vickers," Eddie grunted as he tried to keep from sliding back and forth. "I knew something was up with that guy."

"Don," Beth added, sounding nervous. "Laura called—she's been trying to reach you. Madison hasn't come yet after school let out..."

Donald slammed on the gas, sending the car skidding again around a tight turn.

"Oh my god!" Madison Avery screamed. Marcus tried to shield his eyes, but couldn't make himself look away. The power of Adratheon had almost always been a fantasy of his, something to aspire to beyond all the things he could already have in his own reality.

Something unattainable.

Mythic.

Even when he formed the Remains with the sole intention of carrying on his father's work of harnessing the Cult of Alternus' power, part of him never thought he would truly witness the exact nature of Adratheon.

And now that he had, all he wanted to do with the last moments of his life was to try and grasp it. Everything the Vandrels had done had led him to this, and Marcus knew it all depended on him.

Rachel Kraft lay motionless on the floor, her head a bloody ruin. Benjamin's son was in even worse condition; the boy's entire torso was bent sideways and his head was twisted backward. Marcus couldn't even tell if the kid's skull was still attached to his body.

Marcus allowed himself to look away from the dead kids for a mere moment to see if he was still being held at gunpoint. Barry Vickers was on his back in a pool of blood. He had been standing directly behind Rachel Kraft when Cliff had shot her, and each round found a home in enough of Barry's vital organs to put the tormented man to rest.

While the two teen girls broke into hysterical sobs and the sheriff's kid let out a dozen raging curses while tearing at his hair, Marcus' gaze went between Rachel and Barry. Something about their lifeless bodies triggered an understanding in him, and he realized that Adratheon always needed the girl; maybe not just because she was a Kraft, but simply because she carried the stain of Adratheon's power.

He moved swiftly to grab the gun from Barry's lifeless hand and then stood up to aim at Madison and Cassandra.

"I need one of you in the circle to stop this."

"Stay here," Donald shouted, slamming his door shut.

"Fuck that," Eddie growled, stumbling out of his side of the car. "Bleeding's stopped, man. You need backup if you're going in there."

"Just stay behind me then!"

Together they hurried around to the side of the huge cabin, Eddie limping to keep up, barely staying on his feet. They found the side entrance open and followed the sounds of screams into the basement.

Rachel Kraft stared at her own dead body, knowing that it was what the world outside saw. So much of what she had seen in the past two years made more sense to her now—the principal looking so familiar to her on the first day of school, the teenagers from her nightmares that somehow looked like the popular kids in her school...Her waking dreams had been some kind of vision trying to guide her to this moment.

But the presence she felt inside her that she thought had been her dead aunt—who no one seemed to want to talk to her about—was actually a dark entity that needed her for its escape.

Release me.

The command had followed her from Rhode Island, when dark wings would carry her to high places, leaving her wondering how she had gotten there.

Release me.

Part desperate plea, part prayer, all encompassing.

It was Adratheon's voice, Rachel knew, the dark entity that the secret society in Ransom Creek worshipped. She didn't have time to question these things—as she watched Madison Avery sob, stepping into the circle that had killed the cute boy, Rachel held back the eldritch rage of the vile god looking to escape his bonds.

She was able to convince all of them that she had died, but she wasn't sure how long the illusion would hold.

She just hoped Madison was as brave as she seemed.

Marcus felt the same tingle that came in 1974 when Caroline Kraft descended the ravine. It was as if he were Adratheon made flesh, watching and waiting for the release that had taken eons to finally come. But as he watched Madison Avery timidly step away from her friends, insisting they stay beyond the circle, he was overcome with the knowledge that he now fully understood what needed to be done.

"Adratheon!" Marcus beseeched, reaching out to pick up the largest black candle that would call the dragon from his slumber. "We convene to bask in your infinite presence, and to release your bonds forged in the realm of your own making. We are but humble servants that seek only to extend your reach and—"

"Madison!"

Marcus turned his gun toward the girl. "Don't move! I'll shoot her, Don!"

"Alright!" Donald replied, holding up both hands, his gun hanging loosely in one of them. "You can walk, Vandrel. Just get your gun off my daughter!"

"I got a shot, Don!" The other detective began flanking Marcus.

"Don't!" Donald Avery shouted. "Eddie, stop! That's my fucking kid!"

Marcus kept his gun on Madison, watching for any deception from her or the cops. He was relieved to see they all attended him, waiting for their next command.

"Madison," he said, "all you have to do is repeat after me, and this will all be over."

Madison felt like she was in a dream. Once she stepped into the circle, the world blurred. She was only half-aware that her dad had arrived with his new partner.

Rachel's voice pierced through it all.

"They need me," she said to Madison. "Adratheon can't speak directly to Marcus, because he's not worthy, so he needs me to relay his commands."

Madison tried to speak, but it felt like she was frozen in time; her mouth wouldn't even open. But still, she managed to somehow form words—or maybe thoughts—and asked Rachel, "How are you even talking to me? I saw Cliff shoot you!"

Her surroundings changed then, as if the thoughts she was conveying to Rachel were reacting, the darkness softening.

"We're in a pocket dimension," Rachel's disembodied voice told her. "This is Adratheon's prison, and if he gets out he's going to turn the world into...this."

When Madison heard the name Adratheon, the bizarre surroundings changed again in a way she couldn't quite comprehend; it was as if the mists became sharper and toxic, and Rachel's ethereal voice was accompanied by a rumbling growl from somewhere below.

"If you hear me, Madison, say something!"

The madman's voice was bellowing here, shaking the world.

"I do!" Madison tried to scream, but again her voice made no sound to her ears.

"Good," the man replied. "Your father's going to put his gun down—you too, hotshot! We're going to finish this once and for all!"

"Do what he says," her dad said, his voice sounding almost alien to Madison; she had never heard him sound so afraid of anything.

"Let him believe he's in control," Rachel whispered. "He thinks I'm dead, so don't say or even think my name…"

Madison had no idea how she would accomplish that, but she did her best to clear her mind and just focus on what that psycho was telling her to say.

"Let the kids go," Donald said. "Eddie, take them outside."

Just as Eddie made a move toward the teens, Marcus shouted, "No, Eddie! You stay right there and put your hand on that goddamn candle. That goes for the rest of you. Jared, Cassandra, you're going to fill in for your fathers. Donald, you and your partner will stand in for Jonathan—who didn't have any whelps—and Debbie; her hair was kind of like Eddie's back then."

Donald didn't know Marcus Vandrel that well, but the man seemed to have lost any sanity he may have had. As he reached out to grab the black burning candle, he could see Marcus' face through the hazy veil that occupied the center of the ritual circle.

"Just do what he says," Donald instructed Cassandra and Jared. His daughter's friend was sobbing, but acted on pure survival instinct, for which Donald was grateful. With how crazy Vandrel was acting, he didn't want to take any chances with his daughter's life. "You too, Jared."

The sheriff's son turned a pale face to Donald, and for a moment it looked as if Jared might try something stupid. But thankfully it passed, and he obeyed.

Eddie was the last to reach out for his candle, and he looked at Donald before he touched it. "I don't like this, man…"

Whether it was the blood loss or the insane situation they had found themselves in, his partner's face was a death mask.

When Eddie grabbed the candle, Madison Avery screamed.

Adratheon's laughter was cruel and consuming. Madison tried to scream just to quiet the dark entity's mockery, but she still couldn't hear herself. Rachel was saying something to her, but it was lost in the echoing sound of her father shouting something at Marcus.

Finally, Adratheon quieted and Madison could hear her instructions.

"Tell him you're fine, Madison. Your father is about to do something stupid."

"I'm alright, Dad," Madison lied. She felt some bizarre reassuring presence from Rachel even though she couldn't see her. "What do I do?"

"Tell Adratheon to claim his vessel," Marcus said, his voice sounding more demented than before. "Offer yourself to him!"

"No!" her father called.

"It's the only way she survives this!" Marcus replied. "She saw what happened to Ben's kid! Adratheon will tear her apart unless she submits!"

"You son of a bitch!"

"Don! I can't move my hand!" That was his new partner, Madison realized.

"Yeah, yeah," Jared cried, sounding much less macho than usual. "Mine too! It's stuck!" It sounded like he had started crying.

Cassandra was now screaming for her mom.

"She has to submit!" Marcus hollered wildly over it all. "It can't be stopped now!"

"Rachel," Madison cried.

"Don't say my name!" she replied. "Just say the words. It's the only way."

"But you said we couldn't let him out! You said he'd destroy the world!"

Adratheon laughed again, more subtly, and Madison realized it wasn't Rachel talking to her anymore.

Not knowing what to do, she just said, "I'm sorry, Dad. I love you..."

Eddie watched Donald unleash a bestial roar as he tried to wrench his hand free from the candle, putting his foot up onto the altar for leverage. It was no good.

"Submit!" Marcus screamed. Eddie watched impotently as the man let the submachine gun fall to his side, his attention solely focused on the unreal shit happening in the center of the room. "All that remains will be him!"

That word.

"Madison!" Eddie screamed into the void. "The remains! Walter Kraft's ashes! Get them out of there!"

Marcus didn't seem to hear him. "Submit!" he continued screaming. "Submit to him!"

Madison heard Eddie and pushed herself forward. Even though she couldn't see, it was as if she could feel where the ashes were. Reaching out blindly, her hands grasped what felt like a raised bowl.

Wrapping her fingers around the edges, she used all of her strength to spin and hurl it in the direction of Marcus Vandrel's voice.

CHAPTER 25
BREAKING THE CIRCLE

Eddie was thrown violently from the candle when the storm broke, landing on his right side; the hip with the deeper wound. Despite the pain, he sat up and saw his partner in the grip of a living shadow.

"Don!" Eddie got to his feet only to be pushed up against the wall by something dark and strong. He didn't get a look at the assailant, but he could only assume it was the same thing that was choking Don.

"Dad!" Madison cried, and Eddie was coherent enough to be relieved that she was still alive. Whatever had happened with the ashes had at least saved her. He wasn't sure what he had expected to happen, but after reading about how Walter Kraft died, and the fact that Marcus' little crew seemed so focused on his ashes, it had to somehow be crucial to what was going on. "I can't move," she said. "Rachel said we need to break the circle!"

Donald tried to reply, but the shadowy appendage had him struggling to even breathe. Eddie got up again to help him, but the shadow that had hit him before fell between him and his partner. He looked up at Donald and their eyes met.

Eddie had only known Donald for a few days, but he could already tell what that look said.

Save my daughter.

Looking into the circle, Eddie saw the air still twisting with what could only be magic. He didn't allow himself the rational thought that might have questioned such possibilities. Instead, he focused on how he could get Madison to safety.

"No!" Marcus Vandrel screamed from the far end of the room. Eddie could barely make him out, but could see enough to determine that the man was backed up against the wall and staring up at...

At a fucking dragon.

Madison wanted only to move; just the ability to control her limbs so she could maybe run away from the monstrosity that took shape just a few feet from her.

Adratheon's form materialized from the cloud of ash that Madison had thrown toward Marcus. Black wings filled the high-ceiling basement and a spine of daggers ran down its horned head to its lashing tail. Where he might have had legs or arms, the dragon instead had writhing tentacles that assailed Madison's father and his partner.

In the mere seconds between her scattering the ashes and Adratheon rising from the abyss, Madison had taken in the events through some unknown sensory—sight and hearing were still out of her grasp.

She tried calling for Rachel again, but there was no response. Madison thought these were her final moments, so she allowed herself to just witness Marcus Vandrel's violent demise.

But something strange happened then...

Marcus wept at the sight of Adratheon. The dragon had finally come to him, and despite the circumstances, he allowed himself a moment of reverence under the black god's terrible gaze.

But those eyes conveyed a message to Marcus, one that emboldened him and allowed him to push himself from the wall and step toward Adratheon.

The ashes had broken the circle. He fell to his knees and began scooping up Walter Kraft's remains that had fallen outside the barrier of the candles.

There was still a chance to free Adratheon if he could only—

Eddie turned away, not wanting to watch Donald die, and closed his eyes as he threw himself into the wall of alien energy. He felt wiry hairs against his flesh as he crossed over, and the temperature dropped noticeably. But what nearly drove him to his knees was the terrible sound—like a thousand tortured souls begging for release.

"No!" Marcus screamed again. "Wait! Stay with me!"

Eddie tried to orient himself in his bizarre new setting, focusing on the sound of Marcus' desperate cries; it sounded like he was sucking on his fingers or something as he begged for more time.

"I can finish this," he continued. "I have the ashes—"

Whatever Marcus hoped to say was cut off by another unnatural roar that shook Eddie to his knees.

"Madison!" He struggled to regain his balance. "Where are you?!"

"She's over here," a different voice called—one that was familiar to Eddie but he couldn't quite put a face to it, especially in the strange miasma surrounding him. But he moved toward it anyway.

He hadn't even taken two steps when the haze suddenly cleared and Eddie was face to face with a fucking monster. It opened its jagged maw and spoke in a tongue Eddie couldn't hope to comprehend, but somehow the sounds conjured a warning in his mind.

The girls are mine; leave while you can.

Eddie ignored that and convinced himself that the terrible dragon's maw only existed in his mind. Unfortunately, as he tried to push his arm through its long black teeth, the jaw snapped close and those teeth ripped a long gash down his forearm.

"Fuck!" Eddie threw himself from the creature, grinding his teeth against the pain. "Madison!"

"Don't touch her!" Marcus screamed, his voice sounding right next to Eddie. "Let me finish this! Adratheon! I have the remains! I have—uck."

Eddie heard the unmistakable sound of someone's throat being crushed, and he moved quickly toward where he had heard the familiar girl's voice. Even before he realized who it was, he called, "Rachel!"

"Here!"

A hand reached out and grabbed Eddie's wrist. That touch restored Eddie's vision and he was once again in Vandrel's basement. He saw

Marcus on his knees in the center of his ritual circle, his eyes rolled back in his head as his hands shoved handfuls of Walter Kraft's remains into his mouth. The choking sounds he made sounded like the dragon's growls.

"We need to get him out of the circle," Rachel said, pulling at Eddie's arm. "Grab Madison's wrist!" He whipped his head toward her and saw Rachel trying to move Eddie toward the frozen form of Madison Avery. Donald's daughter looked completely entranced by Marcus' grotesque display. Eddie obeyed and grabbed Madison's arm; she immediately snapped out of whatever had locked her in place.

"Come on!" Rachel said, taking Madison's hand and leading her toward Donald, who looked like he was finally freeing himself from the black tendril that had been strangling him.

"Get Marcus," Rachel called over her shoulder at Eddie. "If he gathers enough of the ashes, he can finish freeing Adratheon!"

Not knowing what the hell the girl was talking about, Eddie looked back at Marcus. He could hear Donald behind him calling for his daughter, but he tried to focus on making sure their only remaining lead for this insane case survived this even more insane situation.

Marcus had begun convulsing by the time Eddie reached him, and when he grabbed the man by the shoulder, Marcus' eyes snapped back down on Eddie. But they were no longer his—they were onyx orbs.

"Take your whores and go," Marcus growled. Eddie imagined it was how a demon might sound, and the words reverberated in his chest painfully. But he kept his grip.

"On your feet," he commanded, pulling on the man's shoulders with both hands now. But some force kept him in place.

"Go!" Marcus growled, a black tongue lashing out from his ashen mouth. The shadowy snake struck Eddie in the shoulder, and, in shock, he looked down to see it was like a spike impaling him.

"Eddie!" Donald screamed. "Get down!"

Letting out an agonized howl as the pain exploded through his chest, Eddie put all his body weight to his right side, hoping to force the man's unnatural tongue out of his body; however, it felt like all he was doing was widening the wound. Somehow he still managed to clear the way for Donald.

Eddie heard the gunshots, followed by what sounded like a thousand shattering panes of glass.

And then he heard nothing.

CHAPTER 26
ECHOES

The dreams were so real, Madison wasn't sure which parts were memory. She knew that the events in the basement of the cabin actually happened, but the specific details were about as blurry as her waking vision.

She could tell she was in a hospital room, but the figure in the chair was a fuzzy blob. She reached up a hand—which was incredibly sore and restricted by an IV—to rub her eyes. She could see now that it wasn't a figure; it was two figures.

Her parents looked asleep.

Madison badly wanted to wake her father up and thank him for coming to save her, but seeing her mother's head resting against his shoulder... She decided instead to lay her hands on her stomach and face whatever terrors awaited in her dreams.

She would face them smiling.

Eddie thought he had already died and gone to Hell, so when he awoke to a crusty, aching pain, it felt sweeter than it should.

But not as sweet as his view.

"Hey, hero."

Tori Kraft smiled down at him, looking more beautiful than ever. Her daughter was beside her, giving Eddie a shy grin as she kept herself partially obscured by her mother.

"Did I die and go to Heaven?" Eddie asked, his voice gravelly. "Not sure why else a couple of angels would be hovering over me."

"Good one, partner," came a voice to the side. Eddie turned to see Donald Avery with his daughter, Madison.

"Super corny, man," she said with a smile.

Donald asked, "How you feeling?"

"Like I got into a fight with a fucking dragon," Eddie said, reaching up to touch his brow.

Rachel let out a restrained giggle.

Eddie looked her way, but the girl's face gave no indication that she had made a peep.

"Rachel told me you saved her from Principal Vickers and that Vandrel scumbag," Tori said in a serious tone, placing a gentle hand on Eddie's right shoulder—the one that wasn't covered in medical junk. "I don't know what happened down there, Eddie, but we owe you everything." She gave Donald a brief glance. "Both of you," and then to Madison, "all three of you."

"It was a team effort," Eddie said, trying to shift slightly until he felt how stiff his body was. "Jesus, how long have I been out?"

"Almost forty hours," Donald said, motioning for Eddie to lay back. "Doctor wants to check you out again, but the surgery went well."

"What the hell happened in there?" Eddie was asking himself more than anyone else in the room. Everything after his stupid knife fight with the Rothen merc felt like a drunken haze.

"Hey, Tori," Donald interjected. "Would you go look for Dr. Stone real quick?"

"Sure," she replied, still holding Eddie's gaze. "Be right back."

He briefly squeezed her hand before she left with Rachel.

"You don't remember anything?" Donald asked when the Krafts were gone.

Eddie shook his head. "Not really. Please tell me we got Vandrel though."

Donald gave his daughter a quick glance before nodding. "Yeah, we got him in custody. But...not sure how much good it'll do. He's... Well, he's not quite himself anymore."

Eddie closed his eyes and groaned. "This place, man..."

"I don't remember anything either," Madison said. "But my dad said you saved me."

Eddie peered at her though half-lidded eyes, not able to hide his smile.

"Thank you," she said sweetly. "Mom said you have to come to dinner at our place now. Those are the rules."

Eddie laughed, and even though it hurt, he didn't let it show.

"Rest up, partner," Donald said. "We'll worry about work later, alright?"

Eddie gave a weak nod before closing his eyes.

Later, after some poking and prodding from the doctor and nurses, Eddie was left alone again. But Tori came in by herself that evening.

"Sorry to bother you again," she began as she crept into his room. "I had a break at work and wanted to check in."

"Definitely not a bother," he said with a smile. "How's Rachel?"

"She's staying at Madison's. Don't think I'll be able to leave her home alone for a while after all of this. But that shouldn't be a problem after tonight."

Eddie gave her a confused look.

She sat in the chair next to his bed. "I'm quitting The Narrow House. Tonight's my last shift."

"Oh," Eddie said, trying to hide his disappointment. He supposed he shouldn't be surprised that she'd be leaving this place after everything that happened.

"With the inheritance and all, I can probably get away with not working for a while."

Eddie flinched. "The manor?"

Tori nodded. "Yeah, turns out, that whole trust in my grandfather's will wasn't properly notarized or something. Someone from the city council heard about what happened and came to the bar, explained everything. I guess one of the victims—Benjamin Windsor—was the city planner and got involved in some real estate matters that didn't really concern him." She shrugged. "Anyway, we're getting everything. So we can move in next week."

Eddie couldn't hide his shock. "You're going to live there?" It was an incredible property, but her daughter had witnessed a brutal murder in there.

Tori nodded, as if expecting his surprise. "My family has a pretty fucked up past here," she began. "But Rachel and I had a long talk, and neither of us want to be scared away from our home." She looked into Eddie's eyes. "Rachel insisted we stay." And then she smiled and took his hand. "But I was easily convinced."

That night, Donald went back to the hospital for another visit.

Marcus Vandrel had three guards; one posted outside his room, one at the only elevator to his floor, and then one at the hospital's main entrance.

Donald entered the room alone, only slightly bothered by the man's eerie giggling.

"Evening, Marcus," he said, dragging a chair over to his bedside. "Feeling any better."

"I am anointed," he tittered, staring at the nothingness that dwelled in the room's ceiling. "Does it get better than being touched by the master of Alternus, Detective?"

"Suppose not. You ready to talk about what happened at your cabin the other night?"

Marcus actually turned his head this time to look at Donald. His white hair had become wiry and chaotic, making him look less like a noble lord and more like some doomsaying pariah.

"You will never comprehend what happened, Donald Avery. It took me my entire life and more sacrifices than you'll ever know to achieve the level of understanding I have now." He looked back toward the empty ceiling above. "You simply cannot fathom what happened."

"Lucky me," Donald replied, sitting back in his chair. Feeling at a loss, he took another approach. "Maybe I can fathom what happened to Caroline Kraft."

Marcus, who had been giggling again, stopped at the mention of Caroline's name. His body became still as if he had just suddenly died. After almost a full minute, Donald was about to get up to fetch a doctor when Marcus finally showed a sign of life by blinking.

"Was it her?" Marcus whispered, but his eyes still focused on something that simply was not there.

Before Donald could respond, Marcus jerked in the bed, his shoulders pinned down by some force as his neck stretched upward. Donald sprung to his feet and drew his gun, but there was no one else in the room. Black marks formed on Marcus' neck as the man tried to scream but couldn't make a sound.

"Help!" Donald cried, aiming his gun at the madman being strangled by nothing. He heard the door slam open behind him and when the lights came on, Donald was momentarily blinded.

"What is it?!" the guard asked.

When Donald's vision focused, he just saw his gun pointed at Marcus Vandrel, who was covering his face, sobbing into both of his mangled hands.

CHAPTER 27
SETTLING

"Shit!" Donald instinctively tried to shake the oil off his hand like it was some attacking insect. Laura quickly grabbed his wrist and used a towel to wipe it away.

"You always panic," she said, but there was no annoyance in her voice. And she held onto his wrist longer than she needed to. She looked up into his eyes and said, "You're going to burn those."

Donald returned his attention back to the skillet full of plump meatballs swimming in a shallow pool of popping oil.

"Hey, chef," Eddie called through the kitchen window, "Anne out here said you have the good bourbon hidden away somewhere."

"That's at my place," Donald called over his shoulder. "There's beer in the fridge out in the garage though."

"I'll grab some," Madison called, leading Rachel from her bedroom.

"No you won't," Laura said. "Not for another five years. Let me grab them." She placed a hand on Donald's shoulder as she added quietly, "Is our daughter seriously almost twenty-one already?!"

Donald smiled and turned over a meatball.

"Can I give you guys a hand in there?" Tori asked.

"Actually, yeah," Donald said, handing her the metal tongs. "You mind taking over. I needed to talk with Anne for a second."

"Need me for that?" Eddie asked.

Donald motioned for him to stay seated in the bar stool. "You don't move! Let those stitches heal, man. Keep an eye on the ladies in there."

He found Anne out in the den, still pouring over the manuscript that was salvaged from Vandrel's basement—which was also excluded from the catalog of evidence in the official police report.

"Make anything of it?" Donald asked, taking a seat next to his old partner.

Anne shook her head slowly, turning another page over onto the small stack of blank, face-down papers on the coffee table.

"To tell you the truth, Donald, I don't know if I *want* to make anything of this. I might turn out like Vandrel." She gave him a sideways look. "What'd you see down there?"

The black appendage that burst from the swirling mists in Vandrel's basement appeared in his mind, and his throat tightened. But all he said to her was, "I'm still trying to figure that out." He motioned to Jonathan Keene's unpublished book. "After reading some of this... I don't know, Anne. I feel like maybe I'm losing it..."

"Dad!" Madison called from the kitchen. "Eddie's never had tomato sauce!"

"I said I *have* had it, I just don't remember what it tastes like!"

Donald looked toward the activity in the kitchen, where Laura had just returned with a cold six pack of beers she was distributing to Tori and Eddie. When he looked back at Anne, she was tucking the manuscript back in the accordion file.

"Let's deal with that later," Anne said, giving Donald a smile that was maybe the most genuine expression he had ever seen on the woman's face. "We have plenty of time."

Donald got up to follow Anne into the kitchen, but something caught his eye on the small desk Laura kept near the dining room table. It was the envelope containing the divorce papers. He couldn't help himself from picking the packet up and then opening it; the signed papers had not been filed yet.

Carrying the documents into the kitchen with him, he held them up for Laura as she brought him a beer.

"You gonna file these?"

She grabbed the envelope from Donald's hand and replaced it with the beer. Tossing the papers onto the kitchen's little side table that was colloquially known as the "junk table," Laura looked at him with a serious, level gaze and told him, "Not yet."

Donald cracked his beer, spraying his otherwise unblemished blue tie. But instead of wiping it clean, he looked over to Eddie, who had been smiling and joking with Rachel Kraft.

The partners locked eyes and offered each other a small toast before returning to the night's revelry.

Later that night, Anne Warren smoked her cigar alone outside, insisting that Donald spend time with his family and new partner.

She watched from the back porch, smiling as she observed the happy couples and the safe teen girls playing cards.

Kneeling down, she opened the accordion file and drew out the manuscript that she knew held the answers to what truly happened in 1974. She tucked the stack of papers under her arm and, page by page, she used the end of her cigar to turn Jonathan Keene's revelations to ash.

Somehow, Anne knew that the answers she spent over twenty years trying to get would not satisfy her anyway.

In fact, the world would be better off never knowing who the hell Adratheon was or what his disciples did in his name.

Besides, she thought, taking a long, final drag on her cigar as she watched Eddie Rane say something that caused Tori Kraft to hug him while laughing hysterically, *some remains just weren't worth remembering*.

EPILOGUE

The handsome man who had strangled Patrick Larson—and likely each of the other Remains—only visited Marcus at twilight.

The Wainwright Clinic issued a lights-out promptly at 7 p.m. every night, and by 7:05 the whispers would come.

"It won't be long, Marcus," the handsome man said, his British accent both intoxicating and dreadful. "I suspect you won't be imprisoned here much longer." He laughed at that—gently at first, but soon his laughter caused Marcus to roll over in his bed and cover his ears.

"Oh, you're such a cunt," he said. "Look, I don't exactly prefer your company either, but you're the one that called me—or whatever aspect of me is still tethered to those meddling Krafts. You think I want you coming into the Revery? It's taken me fucking aeons to tidy this place up, and you people keep stumbling here and mucking up plans."

"What plans?!" Marcus exploded, rolling back to face him. "You haven't done shit! You say you're some big shot in the music industry, but who the fuck has ever heard of Devon Andrews or Unknown Oath?!"

The man looked offended. "You haven't heard of Unknown Oath? Christ, man. Do you guys even get the radio out here?"

Marcus ignored the strange indignation. "Just tell me what you want from me! I'm sick of you dragging me into this—whatever it is! You could have killed me in the hospital, and now I wish you would have—I cannot stand listening to you anymore!"

Devon gave him a strange look, as if he were trying to decide what to make of such a bizarre outburst.

"Look," he finally said, taking a seat next to Marcus on his bed—the cushion didn't sink down because he wasn't really there. "If you're still sour about that whole show I put on for the cop, I'll show you how remorseful I feel about that by doing something I never really do…"

Cautiously, Marcus glanced at him from the corners of his eyes.

"I'm sorry," he said. He waited for Marcus to respond, as if he had just shared an ancient secret.

Marcus just shook his head, hoping to wake up soon. "Just please, leave me alone."

"Afraid I can't do that, Marcus. I'm going to need you for one last trick. I suspect you'll have a visitor in a day or two, and she will offer you a glorious solution to your problem. It seems my efforts with DeMono Tech only partially restored me—if goddamn Walter Kraft would have just…" Devon took a deep breath; it sounded like the dragon's roar from the cabin basement, and Marcus shivered.

"Well," Devon continued, "what's done is done. Anyway, DeMono Tech has the arcane infrastructure in place, but Rothen has the drugs needed. Thanks to Roger buggering the deal with Rothen, they are on their way to deliver what we need."

Marcus looked back up to him. "What do we need?"

"They call it Nexaphane," Devon said, pacing the room now—he seemed to disappear and reappear as if reality were glitching for Marcus, even though he knew he'd left reality far behind. "They've been perfecting this little pill that allows your kind to," he made a motion with his hands as if he were juggling invisible balls, "I don't fucking know…merge with Alternians. It's exactly what we need to get me back to Laramie."

Marcus was completely lost. "What's in Laramie?"

But Devon was gone.

Two days later, Marcus Vandrel was escorted into an empty room where he waited alone for almost an hour.

Finally, a beautiful woman in corporate attire walked in. She had a visitor badge and a leather binder.

"Thank you for waiting, Mr. Vandrel." She took a seat across from him. "My name is Lydia Thompkins with the Rothen Corporation."

"Roger's contact," Marcus guessed aloud. "You had him try to kill me."

"Yes," Lydia said absently as she opened her binder. "He made quite the spectacular mess of it, didn't he?" She looked up and actually smiled at him. "I'll cut to the chase, Marcus—can I call you Marcus? We have reason to believe that you're suffering from a condition that has afflicted many people in Ransom Creek. Mostly unreported and largely undiagnosed."

"What condition?" Marcus asked, but he assumed he could be suffering from any number of psychotic conditions.

Lydia tilted her head. "The best way to describe it might be temporal-personality disjunction. Which is mostly a fancy way of saying you suffer from memory gaps, identity confusion, and perception shifts, especially with your surrounding environment."

Marcus tried not to laugh, but in his head Devon already was.

"I've come here to advise that you begin treatment immediately on our experimental drug Nexaphane, which has been in clinical trials since 1968." Lydia produced a piece of paper and slid it toward Marcus with a pen. "Just sign this consent and Rothen will provide the medication free of charge."

Marcus didn't read it, and he tried to tune out Devon's voice, which urged him to sign immediately. "This drug's been in trials since the 60s and I'm supposed to just assume it won't kill me or make me worse?"

Lydia's face remained neutral as she shook her head. "No, you're supposed to take it so we can see what happens to you." She motioned to the empty room. "Unless you want to stay in this asylum for the rest of your life?"

Marcus looked at the paper again, the words just jumbling together to form Adratheon's name spelled hundreds of times.

"What's the worst thing that's happened to someone taking Nexaphane?" He picked up the pen, knowing he didn't have a choice.

"We believe our last test group in the 80s became lycanthropic, but we're still looking into that."

Marcus meant to laugh at that, but he just wept as he clumsily signed his name.

In his head, Adratheon roared in triumph.

THE END

FREEZE!

YOU HAVE THE RIGHT TO SCAN
AND LEAVE A REVIEW!

ABOUT THE AUTHORS

Adam Sadler (pictured left) and his twin brother

Adam & Brady J. Sadler are the dysfunctional duo
behind over a dozen tabletop game designs, a singular
fantasy metal band, and possibly a few novels.

Adam lives a quiet life in Indiana with his wife
and daughter, where he likes to paint miniatures,
play games, and eat macaroni & cheese.

Brady lives down the
street from him.